MAT THORNE

.

DIAL M FOR...

TERLION BOOKS

For Sally

TERLION BOOKS
P.O. Box 81854
Pittsburgh, PA 15217

This book is a work of fiction. Names, characters, places, and
incidents either are products of the author's imagination or are used
fictitiously. Any resemblance to actual events or locales or persons,
living or dead, is entirely coincidental.

First Terlion trade paperback edition February 2021

LIBRARY OF CONGRESS CATALOG IN PUBLICATION DATA
Names: Thorne, Mat, author.
Title: Dial M for mutants! / Mat Thorne.
Series: The Midnight Extra.
Description: Pittsburgh, PA: Terlion Books, 2021.

Identifiers: LCCN: 2020922921 | ISBN: 978-1-7361682-0-2 (pbk.)
| 978-1-7361682-1-9 (ebook)

Subjects: LCSH Journalists--Fiction. | Horror. | Horror tales. |
Science fiction. | Mystery fiction. | BISAC FICTION / Horror |
FICTION / Science Fiction / Humorous | FICTION / Thrillers /
Supernatural | FICTION / Mystery & Detective / Amateur Sleuth
Classification: LCC PS3620.H7673 D53 2021 | DDC 813.6--dc23

Printed in the United States of America

www.midnightextra.com

MUTANTS!

I

THE MIDNIGHT EXTRA

HER OFFICE smelled like the bathroom of a seedy bar. The endless cycle of cigarettes. That urinal cake perfume. A headache was already forming somewhere deep in Buck's skull and one whiff of her office was just enough to set it alight. He slumped into the old floral sofa across from her desk and sighed.

She watched him a long, silent moment, then returned to the open tabloid on her desk. She clicked her tongue and scratched notes all across the page. Buck sat too low in the sofa to see what she wrote. He didn't need to. Her expression told him everything he needed to know.

"Have a smoke," she said, nodding to the pack of Viceroys on the table.

Buck sat up and took one.

"Why the hell not," he said. "Just why the hell not."

He tapped the cigarette on the desk and hesitated. The chaos of the newsroom sounded through the open door. Phones ringing, voices arguing, the occasional burst of laughter.

"You want me to close that?" Buck said.

"Leave it open."

Buck pressed the cold cigarette to his lips and held it there. "That's what I thought," he mumbled.

She sat the paper down and flattened out the creases with her knobby hands. Just skin and bones and a glitter of cocktail rings moving slowly, tenderly, over the edges. She made a real show of it. She even squared it to the edge of the table and patted it like a puppy.

"This is trash, hun," she said.

Buck lit his cigarette and smiled. "You're the publisher."

She smiled back. Red lipstick smeared across her teeth.

"Not the paper," she said. "The Midnight Extra is an award winning publication." She thumbed toward the wall of gilded plaques behind her desk, then raised her voice to be heard well beyond the office. "Award winning!" she shouted. Then to Buck: "It's your section dear. It's trash."

Buck heard the commotion in the newsroom begin to die down. He could feel their faces turning.

She spun the paper and tapped it with her pen. Buck couldn't help but notice the frowny faces she had drawn all over the *Can You Believe It?!* page. They covered it entirely.

"Subtle," he said.

"Read that headline to me. The banner."

Buck glanced over the page. "Hellhounds from Outer Space," he said.

"Louder."

He looked at her and sighed. He cleared his throat.

"Hellhounds from Outer Space!"

She raised a painted eyebrow. "And you don't see a problem with that?"

"I thought it sounded snappy."

"Snappy?"

"Yeah, snappy. Guy saw an alien that looked like a dog. 'Space-dog' didn't cut it. Sounded like a cartoon character or something. I don't see the problem."

"You don't see the problem?"

Buck looked over the headline again. He checked the spelling, then shook his head. "Looks snappy to me."

"Buck honey, let's pretend for a second that you aren't stepping on everyone's toes with this shit, alright? Sammy covers UFOs. Doris reports on the devil. Digging into their beats is lazy, but you know that. There's a bigger issue here."

Buck raised his hands in surrender. "I don't see it," he said.

She leaned forward and whispered: "Why, pray tell, would a hellhound come from outer space?"

"Why not?"

She slammed her fist on the table hard enough to send the ashtray tumbling to the floor. "Because they come from hell!" she shouted.

Buck nodded slowly. "Well, I see your point, but…"

"Do you think this paper is a joke?"

"I mean…"

"Tabloid of the year," she roared, her face turning crimson. "Five years running."

Buck looked at the plaques again. Those damn plaques. Five in a row with an empty space already cleared in anticipation of the sixth.

"Nineteen eighty-nine through nineteen ninety-three," she yelled. "And I'll be goddamned if we don't get another one this year. Five years running. And it doesn't happen with trash like this!"

"You don't like the headline, I get it."

She spun the paper around, shaking her head. "And the photos," she said. "My god the photos."

"Well the guy saw the damned thing the night before he called. I can't photograph a memory, now can I? I had to improvise."

"Improvise?"

"Yeah."

"It's a dog wearing a mask, Buck."

"I mean…"

"It's not even a big dog. It's like you put a mask on a Chihuahua."

"It's a Dachshund."

"A Dachshund," she said, pausing to look him up and down. "Is that right? A goddamn Dachshund wearing a mask. And it's blurry. You didn't even get it in focus."

"They're quick."

She looked for the ashtray then snubbed out her cigarette on Buck's photo instead. He opened his mouth to speak and she stopped it with a finger in the air. She looked at the photo again then leaned back in her chair and lit another cigarette.

Buck smoothed out the fabric of his shirt.

"You haven't been to work on time in months."

"I've been chasing leads."

"You've been chasing shots. I can smell the booze from here. You keep missing deadlines. Your writing is lazy…"

"Look Janet, I get it."

"You get it?"

"Yeah, no more hellhounds. Loud and clear."

"Oh Buck," Janet said, "we're way past hellhounds."

She sucked on the cigarette until her cheeks puckered. The cherry burned so bright it reflected in her eyes. She watched Buck without blinking, then blew the smoke out in a long, slow stream. "How long have you worked here?" she asked. "Twenty years?"

"Twenty-nine."

She did the math and smiled. "Nineteen sixty-five," she said. "Now those were the good old days. You remember the good old days, Buck?"

He strained his memory, but came up dry. "It's been a long time," he said.

"Well I remember. You used to be something. A real gumshoe. And now look at you." She gestured to him with a little dismissive wave. "You dress the same, but that's about it."

Buck looked down at his tweed suit and shrugged. "The classics never go out of style," he said.

A shadow fell across the desk and Buck turned to see a young woman standing in the doorway. Her hair was cropped short and she wore acid washed jeans and a black shirt with the sleeves pulled up to the palms. And a nose ring. Buck did a double take when he saw it. He wondered if it was the first one he'd ever seen. She knocked on the doorframe and didn't wait for a response. "Miss Lane?" she said.

Buck laughed at the boldness of her trespass.

Janet peeled her eyes from Buck and stared at the young woman. The cigarette smouldered between her fingers.

"Who the hell are you?"

"Betty Roy."

Janet just sat there.

"Sammy told me to come see you."

"Did he tell you to interrupt me?"

Betty didn't flinch. "He just said to come see you," she said. "I'm the new photographer."

"I didn't know we needed a new photographer."

"You fired David last week," Buck said.

"Which one was he?"

"Tall guy, glasses."

Janet shrugged. Her cigarette went out and she tossed the butt on Buck's photo then lit another one. She dismissed Betty with a little wave of her hand. "Go see the girl at the front desk," she said. "Brittany, or whatever her name is."

"Bethany," Betty said. "And I already spoke with her. Bethany sent me to Tom, then Tom sent me to Jenny, and Jenny sent me to Sammy."

"Then go see Sammy."

Betty cocked her head. "Sammy sent me here," she said.

Janet tapped her nails on the desk. She held her cigarette in her red lips and picked up the copy of *The Midnight Extra* and creased it so the snubbed out cigarettes and their ashes all gathered in a little trench. She tipped the paper toward the trashcan beside her desk and tapped it until everything fell out in a little cloud, then she tossed the paper to the floor at Betty's feet.

"You see that photo?" Janet said.

The paper lay open to Buck's section. Betty picked it up and shook the remaining ashes onto the floor. "What is it, a dog?"

"Hellhound," Buck corrected.

Janet turned to glare at him. "You see it?" she said to Betty.
"Yeah I see it."

"Can you do better?"

"A blind kid could do better."

Janet actually laughed. A dry, smoke-filled cackle that made Buck's skin crawl. He opened his mouth to defend himself, then decided against it. Betty had a point.

Janet's laughter turned into a coughing fit and when she was finally done she leaned back in her chair and smiled. "Brittany, right?"

"Betty."

"Well Betty, I'd like you to meet Buck Vincent. Stand up, Buck. Shake her hand."

Buck took his time. He stood with a groan and held out his hand. Betty took it and they eyed each other with suspicion and shook then turned back to Janet. She sat with her hands clasped on the desk in front of her.

"Old Buck here is at the end of his rope," she said. "He's one lousy story away from the sidewalk. One." She held up her forefinger with this last word, then stuck out her thumb to make a little gun. She pointed it at Buck's chest and fired.

Buck just stood there and took it. Janet said more awful things and he just thought about his pounding headache and the flask in the top drawer of his desk. All that warm whiskey. Hair of the dog. Damn if he didn't need it.

"So I'm going to pair the two of you up and see what happens."

Buck snapped out of it, like he got smacked in the face. "You're doing what?"

"Partners," Janet said.

"I don't need a goddamn partner."

"I don't care. It's done. And you," She turned to Betty. "I can already tell you're not going to fit in around here. I have an eye for the nails that won't pound." She gestured to the wall of plaques. "Do you see all these?"

Betty folded her arms and nodded. "Hard to miss them."

"It takes a lot to win awards like these. If you can squeeze blood out of this old stone," she nodded to Buck, "then you might actually make the cut. I doubt it, but we'll see. Now get the hell out of my office. Both of you. And don't come back with any more trash. You hear me?"

Buck didn't say anything. He stepped past Betty and into the newsroom and straight toward his desk in the far corner. He could feel the eyes of the other reporters watching him. Nosey bastards.

Betty followed him, just a step behind. "Boy she doesn't like you," she said.

Buck ignored her. He reached his desk and loosened his tie with a single jerk then shrugged the jacket from his shoulders and tossed it over the back of his chair. Goddamn Janet. Goddamn nosey bastards. He sat and rifled through the desk drawers until he found a silver flask and a few loose pills of aspirin. He took a drink, then the pills, then another drink. He propped his elbows on the desk and held his head in his hands.

"You ok?"

He raised his head long enough to see Betty sliding a chair next to his own.

"Swell," he said.

Betty just looked at him. The bags beneath his eyes and the

permanent frown lines cut into his jaw.

"Jesus," she said at last. "So you're Buck Vincent."

"The one and only."

He took another drink then screwed the cap on the flask and slipped it into the pocket of his vest. His eyes were still burning from the air in Janet's office and he rubbed at them with the heels of his hands and sighed.

"I remember reading your stuff when I was a kid."

"Sure you did."

"The monster section. Can You Believe It?! I used to love it."

"Flattery will get you everywhere."

"I really did."

Buck opened his eyes.

"Really," he said.

"Yeah."

"Name an article."

Betty just looked at him.

"Any article. From any year. Name me one."

"You think I'm lying?"

"There's been hundreds. Name one and I'll believe that you aren't just as full of shit as everyone else around here."

"Are you always this much of an asshole?"

"That's what I thought," Buck said, rubbing his eyes again.

Betty glared at him.

"Crocodile Boy," she said.

Buck stopped.

"Crocodile Boy?"

"Yeah," Betty said. "He really freaked me out. I didn't swim an entire summer because of him."

Buck just looked at her and shook his head. "Crocodile Boy…" he mused. "Goddamn Crocodile Boy. Now those were the good old days. I haven't thought about him in a long time."

Betty sat with her arms folded. She looked at Buck like she wanted to hit him.

Buck leaned forward in the chair and propped his elbows on his knees and stared at the floor. "It's been a rough day," he said.

Betty's expression didn't change.

Buck was silent a moment. He shook his head then sat upright and fixed Betty with a look that bordered on mischievous. It was the first time she'd seen anything close to a smile come across his face. "Tell you what," he said. "If I introduce you two can we start over?"

"Introduce me to who?"

"Crocodile Boy. Who else?"

* * *

THEY CROSSED the newsroom and turned down a hallway lined with old framed issues of *The Midnight Extra*. Betty slowed to read the headlines as she passed:

ARCADE OPENS PORTAL TO HELL!

LIZ TAYLOR'S DRUG-FUELED SEX ROMP!

BIGFOOT BREAKS UP THE BEATLES!

She stopped at this last one, shaking her head at the image of a towering Bigfoot standing among the band. Above the title was a little starburst holding the words: "A Buck Vincent Exclusive!"

"Hey," she called, "This one's yours."

Buck didn't turn. "A bunch of those are mine," he said.

Betty scanned the other covers for Buck's name, finding it on a handful of other covers:

NIXON CONSULTS WITH THE DEAD!

HALLEY'S COMET CREATES WEREWOLF FIASCO!

"I don't see you on any recent ones," she said.

"It's been a rough year."

"The last one was from like a decade ago."

"Well then it's been a rough decade," Buck said. "Now come on, we don't have all day."

They passed through the hallway and out to a wide room with row upon row of cluttered desks and a small army of people buzzing away in their cubicles.

"What department is this?" Betty asked.

"Advertising. Jesus, hasn't anyone given you a tour yet?"

"Nope."

"They just showed you to your desk and told you to wait?"

"I showed myself to a desk. I don't know if it's mine."

Buck sighed. "This is advertising," he said. "The newsroom is where my lovely desk is, and you probably walked past accounting on your way to Janet's office. Photography is off the main walk.

That's where your desk should be. It's also where the darkroom is as well as film processing. Can you do all that stuff?"

"Yeah."

"Good. Because I sure as hell can't."

They crossed the advertising floor and passed through a room with old orange carpeting and an even older refrigerator. "Here's the breakroom," Buck said. "Label your food and don't look too closely at the microwave. It hasn't been cleaned since the eighties."

Betty nodded.

"And bring your own sponge if you want to clean a mug. That one's about to sprout."

Another nod.

"You rethinking your life decisions yet?"

"A job's a job."

Buck considered the words, but didn't agree. "What paper were you at before this?"

"The Post Herald."

"In Fontaine?"

"No," Betty said, thinking for a moment. "Cascade."

"Huh. Never heard of it. Daily?"

"Yeah."

"What was the circulation?"

"Fifty during the week and ninety-five on Sundays."

Buck nodded. "Well our breakroom is probably a downgrade," he said. "But we got their numbers beat."

He led her toward an open floor with a layout and atmosphere similar to the frenzied newsroom. Gangs of men and women sat taking phone calls and scratching notes at their desks or pounding away at their keyboards. Buck had to raise his voice to be heard. "These are the bastards who get our little rag into every supermarket check-out lane they can find," he said. "Over a quarter million copies a week, if you can believe it."

A large map of the east coast, studded with colorful pins, was adhered to the wall behind an empty conference table. Buck led Betty over to it and tapped it with his knuckle. "If you ever wondered how far your photos might reach, that'll show you," he said. "We make it as far as Boston in the north and Savannah in the south. To the west we hit Louisville, but that's about it."

"Not bad for a little rag," she said.

"No," Buck said. "I guess it isn't."

He led them down another hallway, windowless and cramped. Fluorescent lights flickered and buzzed overhead and the smell of mildew rose from the threadbare carpet pulling away from the walls. "This is part of the old office," Buck said. "Back when this place was a much smaller operation. No one seems to care about these old rooms, so I claimed one a long time ago."

He produced a keychain from his pocket and unlocked a door at the far end of the hallway. The room beyond was windowless and pitch black and Betty waited in the hall as Buck stepped inside. He fumbled a moment in the darkness before finding the wall switch and soon the room was filled with a warm and dusty light.

The room was much larger than Betty was expecting. It was also so crammed full of junk that she could barely see the back wall. It looked like a flea market. A maze of steel shelves lined the walls and formed narrow aisles along the floor and every shelf was spilling over. She went to the closest one and poked among the trinkets stored there. An enameled music box, a rusted sword. An old oil lantern with a red studded font and a polished silver plate attached behind the globe. Betty saw her reflection upside down and distorted in the plate and reached out and took the lantern off the shelf to study it in the light. "What is this place?" she asked.

"Twenty-nine years of bullshit," Buck replied from the next aisle over. "Every haunted doll, cursed sword, possessed book, or evil lamp that ever graced the pages of the *Can You Believe It?!* section is stored in this room. I even kept all the masks and costumes and props. You name it. If it was ever in an article, it's stashed somewhere in this room."

"Everything?"

"Yeah, I'd say so," he said, peering through the shelf to see Betty studying the lantern. "You're holding the Lamp of Ptolomy right now. Said to hold the ghost of Cleopatra herself."

"They had oil lamps in ancient Egypt?"

Buck said nothing in reply. Betty could hear him grunting with some unseen effort, then the sound of something heavy sliding along the floor. Then a shuffling. A rattle of chains.

"Buck?"

She heard the door close somewhere in the room behind her. Then the click of the light.

"Buck!"

Total darkness. She still held the lamp in both hands and when she went to set it back on the shelf she found herself colliding with something heavy and rough just as the light clicked back on.

The face watching her was enormous. The eyes like pits, jet black and set deep in a gnarled head of scales. The mouth stretched nightmare wide and the teeth were jagged and spilling from the awful pink of the gums. Its expression was frozen in menace. Hunger and nothing else.

Betty screamed in delight.

"Crocodile Boy!" she shouted. "Yes!"

Buck was clearly disappointed.

"Oh like you weren't going to do something stupid like that," Betty said. "Come on."

"Yeah well, I figured it was as close to hazing the rookie as I could get."

Betty grabbed the latex mask from Buck and turned it in the light. "Oh man he is excellent!" she said.

"He's a little worse for wear these days."

"Just makes him more fierce," Betty said. "Battle damage."

"You know that was based on a real story. A real lead."

"Seriously?"

"Sure was," Buck said. "A fisherman in Georgia swore up and down about it. Never let it go. He called my desk for years, asking if I had any news." He looked down the aisle and nodded to the shelves. "A lot of those old stories came from actual tips and eye witnesses. Most of them, come to think of it. I mean the photos are mostly fake, and a lot of the fluff, but the bones were there."

Betty handed the head back to Buck who placed it carefully in an old wooden trunk. He covered it with a blanket before closing the lid and sliding everything back beneath the shelf.

"Most of them?"

"What?"

"You said most of the photos and stories were fake. Were there ever any real ones?"

Buck raised his eyebrows. "Real monsters?"

"Yeah."

Buck laughed to himself. "Oh Betty I hate to tell you this. Monsters aren't real."

There was a knock at the door, hard and impatient. A man's voice called out as the knob turned. "Buck, you in here?"

"Hey Sammy."

The door opened to a short man wearing thick dark glasses and a obvious toupee. He looked exhausted.

"Damn it Buck I've been all over the building looking for you. All over. Here, take this."

He handed over a piece of paper with a name and number scrawled across it. "That woman has called the floor a hundred times since the issue went out," he said. "She's driving me nuts. Says she needs to talk to you. Says it's important. Life and death."

"Life and death?"

"Yeah, you're gonna love it. She says she's found your hellhound."

Buck raised his eyebrows. "That right?"

Sammy laughed. "Sure is. And get this..."

He leaned in closer, lowering his voice.

"She says it ate her husband."

II

MRS VIVET

THE NEIGHBORHOOD was pretty, in a suburban sprawl kind of way. Lawnmowers always at-the-ready. Fleets of moderately priced sedans tucked neatly into well-swept garages. Every hedge trimmed neat. Every fence freshly painted. All picture perfect, save one lonely house tucked away at the far end of a winding cul de sac, looking for all the world like it had been abandoned for years.

Buck parked his Volvo at the end of the driveway, but left the engine running. He checked his notepad, then looked up to the number on the mailbox. "Looks like the place," he said.

Betty was rummaging through the console, picking up the cassette tapes she found and looking at them with her nose wrinkled. "You've heard of CDs right?"

"I already have the tapes. You think I should buy all those again?"

Betty checked the names and shook her head. "No," she said. "Definitely not."

"Some punk is gonna look through your music in thirty years and make the same face, you know."

"Maybe."

"Definitely," Buck said.

He looked back to the house. Single story and unremarkable, like one of those Sears Modern Homes from the thirties. Brick veneer, attached garage. It was set far back from the road and the sprawling, neglected front lawn had grown into a wild meadow. The eave above the front porch was slanted and on the verge of collapse.

"You seeing this?" Buck said.

Betty tossed the cassettes back into the console. "Looks like a perfect place for a hellhound attack," she said.

Buck grunted a reply and wrote a few things down on his notepad. He looked back up to Betty and tapped the pen on the steering wheel. "Well?" he said.

"Well what?"

"Get a photo."

"From here?"

"Yeah, and be quick. I don't want to sit here any longer than we have to."

"We're not going inside?"

"Why the hell would we do that?"

Betty just looked at him.

"What's the problem?"

"Well it's gonna be a shitty picture for starters. Look how far away we are."

"Don't you have a big telescope lens or something?"

"Telephoto. And yes, but it's still just a picture of a house."

"It'll be enough to get Janet off my back," Buck said. "That's all I care about. Get the shot and we can get the hell out of here. Maybe head to the pound. I bet they'll have a big mean dog we can photograph. A Doberman or something."

"You don't want to talk to that woman?"

"Of course not."

"But she saw your hellhound."

"There is no hellhound," Buck said. "I made it up. I make all of this shit up. I thought that was clear."

"Well something ate her husband."

"Nothing ate her husband, trust me. You have no idea how many bullshit calls I've taken over the years. The number of monster sightings I've followed up on. And do you know how many of those calls led to a real monster? I'll give you one guess."

He made a zero with his thumb and forefinger and held it up to his eye.

"Now just get the damn photo."

Betty didn't budge. "You're a real peach," she said. "You know that?"

"I've been called worse."

"I bet you have."

Neither of them noticed the middle-aged woman waving at them from the sidewalk. She wore a matching turquoise track suit and sneakers so white they looked like they'd never touched pavement. Her ponytail swished from side to side as she ran up to the window. She tapped the glass with her wedding ring. Buck jumped at the sound.

"Excuse me," she said. "Excuse me."

She forced a smile as Buck rolled down the window.

"Hi there," she said. "I'm Mrs Turner from next door. Are you visiting Mrs Vivet?"

Betty glanced at the name scrawled on the notepad: Michelle
Vivet. She leaned over Buck and smiled. "Sure are," she said. "Heading up in just a minute." She patted Buck on the shoulder and sat
back in her seat. He gave her a look.

"Oh thank god," Mrs Turner said. "Finally some communica-
tion." She smiled at Buck and then crouched down to look at Betty.
It was clear she was trying to work out the relationship. "Are you
relatives of Michelle?" she said.

Buck said they were from the Health Department and Betty
said they were cousins. It all came out as a jumbled mess and they
looked at each other and Betty shrugged and Buck just shook his
head. Mrs Turner didn't seem to care or notice. She was stealing
looks of the overgrown yard and the house beyond.

"Well I've been knocking on the door and calling for weeks,"
she said. "I haven't heard a word from Michelle. Not a single peep.
I've even left notes. Maybe you two can get through to her."

"You sound worried about her," Buck said.

"Well I'm worried about the state of her yard," Mrs Turner said.
"I think you'd agree that it's just unacceptable for Spruce Valley. We
hold ourselves to a higher standard."

"Spruce Valley?"

"That's the name of our development here."

Buck leaned his head out of the window and glanced around the
cul de sac. He saw no spruce trees, no valley. "It's beautiful," he said.

"And we aim to keep it that way. The neighborhood association
had an emergency meeting about the yard last week. Emergency,
you understand. There have to be consequences."

"Of course," Buck said.

"A yard like that. I mean really. And all those cats. And the screaming. It's disgraceful. My property value is dropping every minute."

"Screaming?"

Mrs Turner was still looking at the yard and shaking her head. "Lord only knows what goes on in that house," she said. "I don't stick my nose in everyone's business, you know. I respect privacy. But I can only tolerate so much."

"You said you've heard screaming."

"Oh god yes. She must watch scary movies at full volume. It wouldn't surprise me one bit. I walk the dogs down this sidewalk every night before bed, right past this awful yard, and I've heard screams like you just wouldn't believe coming from that place. Other noises too."

"Did you call the police?"

"Oh heavens no!" She said. "Police would be the very last thing we'd need here. That eyesore is dropping my property value enough already. We certainly don't need Spruce Valley showing up on the evening news."

Buck watched Mrs Turner a moment then looked back down at his notepad. "What about her husband," he said. "You see much of him?"

"Never," Mrs Turner said. "I never see him. I think he just works all the time. Can't blame him of course. If your wife was that batty you'd stay away too."

"What about hellhounds?" Betty called from the passenger seat.

"Well the neighborhood association only allows cats and dogs," Mrs Turner said. "Fish tanks as well if they're below a certain size, and only if they're for fish. That sounds silly, but the Williams boy across the street had a turtle in one. You can only imagine the trouble that stirred up!"

"I can only imagine."

"Nothing like this yard though."

"I'll be sure to speak with Michelle about it," Buck said.

"Well I'd certainly appreciate that. The whole neighborhood would!"

"I'll bet."

Buck smiled at her and she smiled back and stood for a moment with her hands on her hips, then she nodded and turned to head back home. She passed in front of the Vivet's yard and stopped by a tall patch of grass spilling over the sidewalk. It appeared to be sprouting like wheat. She held out her hands in a gesture of absolute despair before continuing down the sidewalk.

"Cousins?" Buck said.

Betty's camera bag was already in her lap. "Health Department?" she said.

Buck grunted in reply. He watched her take a chrome Pentax camera from the bag and pop the back open to wind in a roll of film. She snapped the camera shut and advanced the film and took the lens cap off and put it in the pocket of her jeans. Then she opened the door of the Volvo and stood on the sidewalk and stretched. A black leather strap with silver rivets hung loose from the camera body and Betty slung the strap over one shoulder and positioned the camera so that it rested just above her hip. She leaned down to the camera bag on the passenger seat and took out a handful of black plastic film canisters and started sliding them into elastic bands on the camera strap like shotgun shells in a cowboy's bandolier.

Buck sat in the driver's seat, hesitating.

"That woman heard someone screaming," Betty said as she slid the last canister in place.

"Yeah, I heard her."

"So what are you waiting for?"

"This isn't our story," Buck said. "We don't investigate. We make shit up and get on with our lives."

"What about all your old stories? Crocodile Boy and all the 'Buck Vincent Exclusives?' You investigated those didn't you?"

Buck didn't answer.

"Well? Didn't you?"

"That was a long time ago."

"So?"

"Things change."

They eyed each other up. Betty standing there on the sidewalk with her camera at the ready. Buck sitting with one hand on the wheel and the other on the keys in the ignition.

"I'll go without you," Betty said.

"Yeah, I don't doubt it."

He took the keys out and opened the car door and grabbed his notepad and pen from the seat. He squinted into the sun and checked his watch. "We were off the clock fifteen minutes ago," he said.

Betty closed the passenger door and and started up the yard.

"And we don't get overtime," he yelled after her, following the trail she made through the tall grass.

They reached the porch and climbed the dry rotted steps and stood beneath the falling eave. Betty tried to peer into the large picture window above a set of rotted chairs, but found the inner curtains drawn tight. Buck just stood a moment, taking it all in. The peeling blue paint and missing planks. Fallen leaves and branches gathered so deep in the crooks of the wicker furniture they sprouted grass. Sun bleached frisbees and the errant baseball gathered near the broken lattice trim at the edge of the yard. Candy wrappers and soda cans and an empty bottle of bubble formula. Flotsam of the suburbs.

He studied the letters plastered to the inside of the storm door. How quickly the tone shifted from neighborly concern to threats of eviction. He pressed the doorbell, but heard no chime from inside the house. Big surprise. He opened the storm door and clicked the brass knocker a few times and waited, then he clicked again. No response. A mosaic sidelite was installed along the door and Buck cupped his hands to the cut glass and peered inside the house.

It took him a moment to understand what he was seeing. Like some trick of the eyes. At first he wondered why someone would dress a mannequin in an evening gown and stand it in their entryway. It was a fleeting thought. A harmless, simple question. What purpose would it serve? He pressed his face closer to the glass and when he realized it was not a mannequin at all but a woman standing there alone in the shadows it made his stomach turn. Just standing there. Motionless in the dark entryway, facing away from him. Her dress so strangely formal, like she was ready for a ball. Her gloved hands drawn up above her waist, delicate and without purpose, like the hands of a cartoon princess.

She just stood there. And Buck thought maybe she didn't hear him, so he knocked again, louder this time, and waited.

"What in the hell," he muttered.

Betty peeled some old paint from the porch with the toe of her boot. When she heard Buck's voice she walked to his side and tried peering through the glass. "What is it?"

"Damned if I know." He tapped on the sidelite with his knuckle. "Ma'am," he said, quiet at first, then louder. "Ma'am? Mrs Vivet? This is Buck Vincent. From The Midnight Extra? I'm here about your hellhound."

Her head jerked toward his voice.

"Mrs Vivet?"

She spun and folded her hands and walked gracefully toward the door. Buck heard the many deadbolts flipping open, one after the other. Then the chain. Finally the handle turned and Mrs Vivet stood there in the dark entryway and curtsied.

"Well good afternoon Mr Vincent," she said with a warm smile. "I'm so glad you've come."

The first thing Buck noticed was the ragged chunk of flesh missing from her lower lip. Nearly half of one side was just gone and through her smile he could see the roots of her lower teeth. He tried not to look. The rest of her seemed to agree with his first impressions. Her hair was perfectly styled and pulled up in a pale blue ribbon. Her dress, in matching blue, billowed out around her. Buck thought that if she'd been wearing a tiara it would look right at home. But that lip...

"Come in," she said. "My goodness come in. You must be so cold."

Buck raised an eyebrow. The day was perfect for June. Maybe even a little hot.

"I'm awfully glad you've come. Awfully glad. Now get in out of the weather. My goodness I'll be glad when this passes. I haven't been out of the house in ages. I can't even remember the last time it's been so long."

Buck stepped through the threshold with Betty following close behind. Mrs Vivet slammed the door behind them with such force it made the wall shake. She latched the deadbolts in quick succession, top to bottom, flip flip flip, then slid the chain back in place. She bowed and rolled her hand to gesture them into the dark living room, then waited for them to sit on the couch before disappearing into the kitchen.

They sat a shocked moment in the silent dark, neither knowing what to say. The heavy curtains behind them were pulled shut and whatever daylight might have slipped in around the edges was swallowed up by the shag carpet and plush victorian furniture. Mrs Vivet seemed to realize this the moment she left and when she reappeared in the kitchen doorway she apologized and smacked her own forehead and reached down to plug in a thick extension cord that snaked along the wall. Immediately, a small forest of floor lamps with missing shades blazed on, filling the room with light. Buck raised his hand to shield his eyes, but the bare bulbs had already drawn little trails across his vision.

"There," Mrs Vivet sang as she disappeared once more into the kitchen. "Much better."

Buck just turned to Betty and waited.

"What?" Betty said.

"You still think there's a story here?" he whispered. "She's a Looney Tune."

"Yeah, and what was the guy who saw Crocodile Boy like?"

Buck turned away. "Perfectly reasonable," he said. "A scholar."

"I bet."

A glass shattered in the kitchen, followed by a "Whoopsie!" from Mrs Vivet and a little giggle. A large, hairy beast of a brown tabby cat ran from the kitchen as she laughed, likely frightened by the broken glass. It made its way along the living room wall before stopping to watch Buck and Betty from the shadows of a cushioned divan. Its yellow eyes moved back and forth between them, back and forth. A second cat, identical to the first, followed after. It sheltered a moment to watch them, then clawed its way up to rest on the back of a velvet armchair, passing in front of one of the floor lamps as it did so, casting a monstrous shadow on the opposite wall. A tiny bell on its collar jingled with the effort. The first cat shook its head in reply, jingling a tiny bell of its own.

Another bell rang from the kitchen, then others from the shadows of the hall. Soon there were no fewer than a dozen of the big, hairy cats all gathered in the living room, each perfectly identical, watching Buck and Betty sit awkwardly on the couch.

"Alright, can we leave now?" Buck asked.

"You afraid of cats?"

Buck locked eyes with one sitting a few feet away on the carpet. It licked its lips.

Before he could say anything, Mrs Vivet entered the room with a floral tea set laid out on a polished silver tray and made her way to the coffee table in front of the couch. The cats parted as she passed. Once the tray was settled she turned to them and smiled.

"I see you met the Stevens," she said. "Well a few of them at least."

"The Stevens?" Buck asked.

She gestured to the strange army of cats. "My little friends," she said. "I swear there's more every day. They just wont stop multiplying! The little darlings. They seem to be quite interested in you two."

"Quite," Buck said as one of the Stevens brushed itself along his leg.

"They're all named Steven?" Betty asked.

Mrs Vivet's head snapped toward Betty. "Hello dear," she said. "I don't believe we've met. I'm Mrs Vivet."

"Hello Mrs Vivet," Betty managed. "I'm Betty Roy."

"And why are you here, dear?"

Betty leaned forward to free the Pentax, then held it up to show Mrs Vivet. "I'm a photographer with The Midnight Extra," she said. "You called us."

"I did!" Mrs Vivet said, clapping her hands together. "Oh I most certainly did." she sat down in a high back chair beside the couch and took a small sip from one of the teacups. "I've only recently been able to use the telephone you know. It was as though I'd simply forgotten how. Isn't that peculiar? I've been looking at it for days and just scratching my head. Scratching and scratching and scratching. It's as though I'd never seen one. And then I saw your article taped to my front door this morning and all of a sudden I remembered how to use it. And so I called you. And here you are."

"And here we are," said Buck.

"Yes, and just in the nick of time. Something awful has been lurking around this house and it wasn't until you described the hellhound in your article that I said to myself, 'That must be what I have!' How fortunate."

Buck tried to think of his hellhound, but all he could picture were the glasses of whiskey it took to cook it up. "Refresh my memory," he said.

"Well you said it was hideous. And that is perfectly correct. Right on the money. You also said it was terrifying and that is very true as well."

Buck wrote the words "hideous" and "terrifying" on his notepad. He waited for more, but Mrs Vivet just smiled at him.

"Anything else?"

"Well let's think," Mrs Vivet said through her jagged smile. "I said it was hideous and terrifying, didn't I?"

Buck looked at her a long moment, then down to his notepad. He tapped the two words with the butt of his pen. "You did."

"Well then I'd say that's a perfect match. Please, drink your tea."

Buck and Betty leaned forward to their tea cups. Both were bone dry. Mrs Vivet's was clearly empty as well, but she brought it up to her lips again and made polite little sipping noises.

"Oh, and also the mouth," she said between sips.

"The mouth?"

"I forget the particulars, but you said it was large and just bursting with teeth. That definitely sounds like my hellhound. It would of course need a large mouth to swallow Steven like it did."

Buck clicked his pen a few times. He nodded to himself.

"Mrs Vivet."

"Yes dear?"

"When you called the Extra this morning, did you tell the man on the phone that a hellhound ate someone named Steven?"

"Of course I did."

Buck slid the pen and notepad into the inner pocket of his sports jacket. "This is starting to makes a little more sense," he said.

"Well that's certainly good to hear."

"It's kind of funny actually. See, the man you spoke to, Sammy, well he thought you said the hellhound ate your husband, not one of your cats. That's why we're here. And I'm sorry to say it, but a dog attacking a cat isn't that newsworthy. It's sad, no doubt about it, but it's not the sort of story we report on. I hope you understand."

Mrs Vivet nodded. "Well I can see the confusion," she said. "The hellhound did eat my cat. Several of them, actually."

"And I'm truly sorry to hear that."

"But my husband is also named Steven. Or was, I should say."

Buck just looked at her.

"And the hellhound ate him too. It gobbled him right up."

She tipped the cup up to her lips again, smiling wide-eyed at Buck the entire time.

* * *

THEY FOLLOWED her as she glided from the living room into the kitchen and to the family room beyond. Buck couldn't get that cartoon princess idea out his head as he watched her. She held her arms out at her sides as she walked, with the fingers lightly extended, like she expected a songbird to perch on one any minute.

She seemed so out of place among the army of hairy brown cats that followed her and the glare of the shadeless lamps. Mrs Vivent noticed Buck shielding his eyes from the light and laughed her polite little laugh.

"I know," she said. "It's awful bright, isn't it? But you know I just keep seeing such terrible things in the dark. I couldn't stand it anymore. These lights seem to do the trick though. I don't think my hellhound likes bright lights."

She led them through the mud room and towards the garage, passing the basement door as she went. Buck couldn't help but notice the large security panel on the wall beside the door. Like something from a bank, or a prison. He stopped a moment to study it. Mrs Vivet stopped as well.

"What the heck do you keep in the basement?" Buck asked, half amused. "Capone's vault?"

The smile was gone from Mrs Vivet's face. She looked at Buck like he was stealing the silverware. "Nothing," she said, the song gone from her voice. "There is no door there. There is no basement."

Buck looked at the door to the basement.

Mrs Vivet smiled again. "This way dears," she sang. "Right this way."

Buck gave Betty another one of those "let's get the hell out of here" looks. She nodded in agreement.

Mrs Vivet opened the door to the dark garage and shivered. Without taking another step she leaned forward and reached her arm around the edge of the door and slapped around until she found the light switch. Her smile never faded. The lights clicked on and she straightened out her dress and led them forward. "Now it's a bit of a mess in here," she said. "But this is where I saw the hellhound. It was right over there, actually."

There was no need for her to point to the broken, twisted metal of the garage door, but she did anyway.

"Over there, where those scratches are."

"Oh my god," Betty said, raising her camera. "Oh man."

Buck stepped onto the empty floor of the garage. He couldn't take his eyes from the shattered door and as he put his foot down it crunched on something small and hard. A tiny little ringing sounded from beneath his loafer, and when he raised his foot he saw that he had stepped on a cat's collar. He crouched down to pick it up, noticing the blood that stained it and the greater streaks of blood along the polished concrete floor.

"Betty," he whispered, holding out the collar and nodding to the blood.

Her eyes widened. She took the collar from Buck and spun it in the light, seeing how it was torn open and frayed.

"Oh my," Mrs Vivet said, peeking over Betty's shoulder. "It looks like it ate one of the cats as well. Oh my my my."

"Mrs Vivet," Betty said. "Don't you think you should call the police?"

Buck shot up from the floor like he was called to attention. He coughed and stood between Betty and Mrs Vivet."

"The police?" Mrs Vivet said. "Oh my."

"She didn't say police," Buck strained. "She said please. Puh-leese."

"Please what, dear?"

"Can you... please get us some more of that wonderful tea?"

Mrs Vivet lit up. Her hands went out once more to their fairy tale pose and she curtsied slightly and spun so fast her hair and dress billowed out around her. "But of course!" she said. "Of course, of course. But I'll have to make another pot. You two wait here."

She hummed to herself as she flitted from the garage.

Buck watched her go, then turned to Betty. "Are you nuts?" he said. "Call the cops now and we lose the exclusive. It's like a siren call to reporters. They're all listening to the scanners."

"Whoa," Betty said. "Where'd you come from? Ten minutes ago you wanted to leave."

"Ten minutes ago I thought this was a wasted trip. Something actually happened here."

"Yeah I can see the blood."

"And you haven't taken a single photo."

"This could be a crime scene, Buck."

He wasn't listening. He was too busy marveling at the twisted angles of the garage door.

"Look at this," he said, walking closer. "I mean look at it. Something tore through this like it was made of paper."

"I see it."

"This could be a real story."

"Hellhounds from Outer Space, Part Two," Betty said.

Buck ran his hand along the split panel and the broken steel hinge. "Nah, no more hellhounds," he said. "I don't know what did this but it wasn't a dog."

"Tell that to Princess Vivet."

Buck stood and wiped his hands on his slacks. "We need to get a better description from her," he said. "Something we can use to make our photo. We can follow up on the husband too. Damn, if we do that and run some shots of that door and that bloody collar. I mean hot damn!"

"I think we can do better," Betty said, peering through the remains of the garage door. "I think we can do a hell of a lot better."

III

STAKEOUT

BUCK TIED the bloodied cat collar to the end of a long spool of twine, then looked around the garage ceiling for a suitable beam on which to drape it. Finding one near the center of the floor, he tossed the collar over and unspooled the twine and set it at the foot of his folding chair, next to the stack of empty tea cups Mrs Vivet continued to serve. Outside, the sun was setting low over the houses at the far end of the cul de sac. A golden streak of light came slanting in through the shredded corner of the garage door.

Betty was setting up her tripod, flipping down the latches along the legs and watching the bubble level until it sat even on the ground. Satisfied, she attached her camera and started to compose the frame.

"I just wanted a couple photos," Buck said, leaning down to watch the sunset through the garage door. "How did I let you talk me into this?"

"It's a stakeout," Betty said. "Isn't that a thing you reporters do?"

Buck had to think about it. "Not this reporter," he said at last. "Not for a long time."

"But you used to?"

"Yeah, I guess. I don't remember."

"So what do you do now?"

"What do you mean?"

"For your stories," Betty said. "You clearly don't like to do interviews or stakeouts or anything else."

Buck thought a moment. "I write most of them at the bar," he said. Then quieter to himself, "Damn near all of them, actually."

Betty slid a large flash into the shoe above the camera's viewfinder. She flipped a switch at the base of the flash and waited for the light to turn orange then pressed a small grey button with the tip of her thumb. The garage filled with a split-second burst of light. She took out her light meter and stood a few feet in front of the flash. "Can you do me a favor?" she asked.

"Sure thing."

"Press that little button on the back of the flash when I tell you to. Ok?"

Buck walked behind the tripod and put a hand on the flash and found the little button. "Got it," he said.

Betty held up the light meter and told Buc to fire the flash. She checked the reading and then walked back to make some adjustments then asked him to do it again.

Buck watched her as she worked. The seriousness of it. How she made tiny adjustments to the focus and frame, how carefully she metered the light.

"You're really into this," he said.

Betty shrugged. "Yeah," she said. "I guess I am."

She pulled another flash from her camera bag and started setting it up on a second, smaller tripod, about ten feet to the side of the first. She ran a cable from the base of the second flash to the camera, then repeated her readings.

"Two flashes?" Buck asked.

"Yeah."

"Well that's two more than I normally use."

"Hit it again."

Another flash of light.

"If you just use the one on top of the camera it makes things look like paper cutouts," Betty said as she changed the angle of the second flash. "This adds depth."

Buck was impressed. He walked over to the spool of twine and pulled it, making the cat collar rise up toward the rafter it was hung over. He jerked on the twine a few times, sending the collar bouncing into the air and making the tiny bell jingle.

"How's that for bait?" he said.

"Perfect."

"You still need me?"

Another flash.

"No I got it from here."

Buck nodded and jingled the bell one more time then set the twine back down beside his chair.

He couldn't help but stare at the blood streaking across the floor.

"Something killed that cat," he said.

"Yeah, and we're going to get a photo of it."

Buck nodded, slowly.

"Probably just a dog," he said.

"Yeah probably."

Another flash.

"And that thing about her husband," Buck said. "That's gotta be bullshit."

"Yeah, it's gotta be."

And that great hole in the garage door. How the metal was buckled and torn away. Peeled open like a tin can. And damn there was a lot of blood on the floor. He kept seeing more of it.

"She must have just crashed into the door with her car," Buck said.

"Yeah," Betty said. "Must have."

"I didn't see a car though."

"Maybe it's in the shop?"

"Yeah," Buck said. "That's probably it."

He walked to the far side of the garage, stopping to look among the sagging plywood shelves. Broken tennis rackets, deflated volleyballs, an old rusted bike pump. He dug through until he found a baseball glove, which he pulled out and examined.

Betty turned from her setup. "You want to play catch?"

Buck tossed the glove on the shelf and dug further, finally pulling out a faded Louisville Slugger. He held it out to feel its weight, then smiled at Betty and mocked a two handed swing.

"Just in case," he said.

Betty looked at the baseball bat in Buck's hands for a long moment.

"See if you can find another one," she said.

"How about a croquet mallet?"

"Better than nothing," Betty said, walking over to grab it.

The door leading to the mud room banged open and Mrs Vivet stood smiling in the doorway. She held the tea tray out in front of her, but there were no cups to be seen.

"Oh you two are just so brave," she said. "So brave. I just can't imagine."

"More tea, Mrs Vivet?" Buck asked.

"Not this time," she said. "This time I've made cookies."

Buck and Betty's ears perked up.

"I've brought all sorts. It took ages to get them ready."

She set the tray down across the arms of one of the folding chairs. Buck peered down to see that it was covered in photographs of cookies that Mrs Vivet had very carefully cut out of her recipe books.

"Now there's raisin oatmeal, macadamia nut, and chocolate chip, of course."

"Of course," Betty said.

"And I was thinking about making the chocolate chocolate chip, but I just wasn't sure how hungry everyone was."

"These will be just fine," Buck said. "Thank you so much."

"Thank *you* so much Mr Vincent. Now if you'll excuse me I see the sun is just about to set and I can't be anywhere near this awful garage when that happens. It's like standing in a graveyard. No thank you. I'll be inside with the Stevens. I don't ever sleep, so just give a knock if you need more tea. I'll leave it by the door."

"You don't sleep?"

"Oh heavens no," she said laughing. "My heavens."

She was still laughing as she closed the door.

Betty nodded to the door. "There's a story right there if this hellhound thing doesn't pan out."

"Suburban Barbie Survives on Air Alone!" Buck said.

"Can you believe it?!" Betty replied.

Buck went over to the tray and held up a few of the cutout cookies. "You have a preference?" he asked.

"I was really hoping for the chocolate chocolate chip."

He smiled and tossed the cookies on the tray.

"Pretty sure I have a couple bags of chips in the car."

"Yes please."

He crouched through the hole and disappeared down the driveway. Betty watched him leave, then went over to the shelf and pulled down an old camping lantern that hung from a metal hook. There was a card table leaning against the further wall and she set the lantern down and dusted off the table and unfolded the legs. She moved Mrs Vivet's cookie tray to the ground and arranged the aluminum folding chairs so they faced the garage door and placed the card table between them. It took a few minutes to prime the lantern, but she got the mantles lit and by the time Buck returned a warm glow was cast throughout the garage. She clicked the overhead fluorescents off and sat down in one of the chairs. Buck sat in the other. The baseball bat and croquet mallet were propped between them on the table.

"Barbecue or plain?" Buck asked.

"Barbecue."

"Good choice," he said, tossing her the bag.

They ate the chips and watched the last sliver of sunlight stretch across the floor before it finally disappeared. The gas lantern hissed quietly on the table.

Betty folded up her empty chip bag and put it in her pocket. Buck crumpled his into a ball and tossed it on the floor.

"You really think she'll fire you if you don't have a good story?" Betty asked.

Buck considered the question. "Maybe," he said. "Maybe she will."

"You worried about it?"

"Nah," Buck said. "Just means I can retire a few years early."

Betty looked at him.

"You're worried."

"Of course I'm worried," Buck said. "That's why we're here isn't it? To go the extra mile? To put another plaque on the wall."

"She's real proud of those plaques."

Buck couldn't help but laugh. "Did you read them?"

Betty shook her head.

"The last five are from the Harold R. Springer Foundation. I'll give you one guess what her husband's name is."

"You're kidding me."

"Nope. And that's husband number three. We had nine in a row from the Burt C. Davidson Group before those."

"Oh man."

"You didn't really think you were working for a standup organization did you? I hate to tell you this, but we peddle in sensational bullshit and nothing else."

Bettty was silent. Buck looked to her and to the camera and flashes she had so meticulously set up.

"But hey," he said. "That doesn't mean you can't have fun while you gather the bullshit. Just don't do it your whole life, alright? There's not much light at the end of this tunnel."

Betty reached inside her jacket pocket and pulled out a worn

pack of Camel cigarettes. She shook one out and offered the pack
to Buck.

"You don't seem like the type," he said, taking one.

"I like to have one with a drink."

Buck made a show of looking around, confused.

"You still have your flask don't you?"

"Well damn," Buck said. "Indeed I do." He opened his jacket
and pulled out the silver flask. He held it between two fingers and
shook it. "Whiskey is good for the nerves," he said.

Betty lit her cigarette and passed the lighter to Buck. He traded
her the flask and they sat a moment with the lantern and card table
between them, watching the great hole in the garage door. A pair
of moths found their way inside and began circling the lantern.
Outside, the deep blue of twilight had turned an even black.

"I was on a stakeout for Bigfoot in nineteen seventy-two," Buck
said quietly.

"I thought you didn't remember any stakeouts."

"Well I just remembered this one. You want to hear about it,
or not?"

"That's the year I was born, you know."

Buck looked at her and did the math. "Jesus," he said.

"You thought I was older?"

"No... it's just. Twenty-two years is a long time. Just doesn't
seem like it's been that long. Damn."

"Makes you feel old?"

"I know I'm old," Buck said. "I don't need confirmation. It's
just. I don't know, sometimes you get reminded of how much time
has actually passed."

"Isn't that the same thing."

Buck shook his head and took another drink.

"No," he said "It isn't."

He screwed the cap back on the flask and set it on the card table. Betty picked it up and took the cap back off.

"You really want to hear some old guy talk about the good old days?"

"Why not?"

Buck looked at Betty for a long moment. How she sat with her feet on the edge of the folding chair with her knees up to her chest and her sleeves pulled down to nearly cover her hands. He wondered about the last time he had really spoken to a twenty-something and realized it may have never happened. "Don't you have somewhere better to be tonight?" he asked.

Betty looked taken aback and Buck held out his hands in apology. "I don't mean that in a bad way," he said.

"If I had somewhere better to be I'd be there," Betty said.

Buck thought a moment and nodded his head. "Yeah me either," he said. "I don't have anywhere better to be."

"So tell me about Bigfoot."

Buck thought a moment and smiled to himself. "There had been a number of sightings up in the Midden Mountains," he said. "Near the national park. You ever been up there?"

"No."

"It's goddamn beautiful."

"You don't seem like much of an outdoorsman to me," Betty said.

Buck nodded in agreement. "I'm not, believe me. It took a lot of bargaining to get me out there. But damn I was glad I went.

People kept seeing Bigfoot and I just wanted to get my costume and shoot some photos and be done with it, you know?"

"You have a Bigfoot costume."

"Of course I do," Buck said, taking a drink from the flask. "It's a good one too."

"Oh my God."

"Well that was the backup plan. So we interviewed all these yokels and honed in on where they were seeing things. Then we packed up and hit the trail. Took plaster of paris and everything. Hoping to make casts of the footprints. You know how heavy plaster of paris is? I mean Christ what a trip. Spent two nights in the woods. First was halfway up the mountain, where the forest was still dense. I remember how dark it got. No light at all after the sun went down, like being in a cave." He thought a moment and shook his head. "That night was scary as hell," he said. "We heard all sorts of noises. Woke up in the middle of the night to what sounded like someone banging two trees together. Just this deep, heavy noise echoing through the forest. My nerves were just wrecked."

"Hope you brought your whiskey."

The trace of a frown crossed Buck's face, deepening his wrinkles. "I didn't need it back then," he said. "I was dry as a bone."

"Did you find any tracks?"

Buck grinned and took another drink. "Plenty," he said. "Size ten."

"You're kidding."

"Nope. We walked all around the camp as soon as the sun came up. Neither of us slept a wink and we got out there at first light and tromped around like a couple of real scientists. Cameras and measuring tape and all that goddamn plaster. We took it seriously. Then we found all those boot prints and just lost it. Laughed our asses off. I went ahead and made an impression anyway. Sort of a way to commemorate the trip."

"Did you turn around and leave?"

"Hell no," Buck said. "It was beautiful out there, weather was perfect, so we went ahead and enjoyed ourselves. We knew Bigfoot wasn't a threat, so we pushed on ahead. Got to the top around sunset. We had been in dense forest for two days and when we got to the ridgeline it all just sort of opened up. I remember laying in the grass and watching the stars while some idiot tromped around in the forest pretending to be Bigfoot. Goddamn, that was a riot. He even started to make these deep howling noises. We said it must have been mating season."

"Who'd you go with?"

Buck was silent for a long time. He took the last drag of his cigarette and blew the smoke out in a slow stream.

"My old partner," he said at last.

"I thought you didn't need a partner."

Buck sighed. "Back then I did," he said.

More moths had joined the circuit around the lantern, sending little flitting shadows all around the garage. Betty took the flask from the card table and drank from it then wiped her mouth with the back of her sleeve. Something about Buck's tone had silenced her. She didn't know what to say.

Buck dropped his cigarette to the cement floor and snubbed it out with the toe of his shoe.

"God that was a million years ago," he said.

* * *

BY THE TIME the last of the lantern's fuel was spent they had both fallen soundly asleep in their folding chairs. Betty beneath an old blue tarp, Buck beneath a canvas grill cover. The hiss of the lantern slowly faded along with the light, dimming and dimming until finally the garage was silent and dark. The circling cloud of moths vanished with the light.

So it was. And when a gnarled face appeared from the broken splinters of the garage door there were no open eyes to see it.

Dark against dark. The waning moon cast some small light on the driveway and it was this faint contrast that gave the thing its shape. The hunch of its stride. The long limbs and long hands.

A wayward moth landed upon Buck's nose and he brushed it away as he slept. Just a thoughtless motion of the hand, but the movement seemed to excite the thing beyond the door and it stooped low and slid itself into the garage.

It made no sound as it crept forward. Hands out before it, fingers splayed.

A scent hanging in the air gave the thing some pause. Heavy scent. Dark and delicious. It reared back its head, causing the jaw to go slack, then began sniffing at the air. Sniffing and sniffing. A bloodhound mania and yes some delight here hanging and the thing reached out a trembling hand until it landed upon a tiny scrap of fabric in the air and began to pull.

The woman in Buck's dream sat on an outcropping of rock along the high ridge of a mountain. A storm stirred miles in the distance. Its fury made the sky and the sunset pink and vivid in a way he had never known in life and he found himself wondering how he had come to be in such a place. Somewhere he did not belong. And when he looked at her again she became suddenly familiar to him and he cried out to her but the storm was now at her back and the mountain she sat upon was a small skiff moored in the ocean. A bronze bell hung at the bow, rocking with the pull of the waves, but its sound was dampened by the storm and it made no great warning, only a restless jingle, tiny among the crashing ocean. He watched how the battered skiff finally came loose of its mooring and slid beneath the water. How she made no effort to abandon it as the water rose to her waist and then her shoulders and then her neck. She only smiled to him and he could only watch. And still the bell rang out. That tiny sound. And as the dream faded around him he could still hear it. Still hear it now in the dark, beneath his grill cover blanket. And he felt the twine wrapping his chair begin to stretch and tighten.

His eyes shot open, but he didn't dare to move. Just his eyes open wide and he heard the jingling and knew it was the bloody cat collar he had hung from the ceiling and he strained in the darkness to see something standing there in silhouette. Standing like a man. But its shape was contorted. Incorrect. That was all he could think. Like a man, but incorrect. He had a moment to think of that. How that simple word seemed to rise up and shout at him. Incorrect. Wrong. The thing he was seeing was wrong.

It sniffed at the collar, tugged at it. Then the wet sound of its tongue, tracing the edges, looking for blood.

Buck turned his head to the tripod and the camera above it. He felt another tug on his chair as the thing pulled again at the suspended collar. Then another tug, slightly harder but unrelenting, until finally the twine snapped.

His flask was somewhere at the edge of the card table. He knew it was. That final disappointing sip when you want more but thats all there is and he had set it just at the edge. The jingling sound grew as the thing lapped at the collar but Buck knew that a hint of old blood would be nothing to the real thing and he had a moment before god knows what so he reached out and tipped the flask over and let it fall to the ground as he slipped out of his chair and grabbed the baseball bat and ran behind the camera.

Betty woke to the sound of the flask. The tarp rustled as she stirred. "Buck?" she said. "Buck?"

The thing bristled with her voice. It screamed out with a wail that sounded for all the world like a creature in pain. A harrowing, tortured cry and Betty kicked out with her feet in panic and sent herself flying backward in the chair.

It was on her at once. One stride and it reached out with those long arms and those long fingers and as it closed them on her ankles the garage filled with a burst of light.

Pop! Light so bright to their night-tuned eyes it hurt to see it. Like watching the sun. And in its midst they saw a thing there crouched with two screaming mouths, open wide and distended.

The light was gone in an instant, making the darkness that replaced it seem all the darker and the thing now just a fading image burned into Bucks vision. Teeth wet and shining.

It cried out again and now the sound was split. One cry low and mournful. The other screeching like a bird of prey.

Another flash of light.

And now its back was turned. The protrusions of its spine clear beneath the sunken flesh. The bald head swollen like a tumor on one side. A bloody cavity in the other.

Another flash and it was gone.

Another flash. Another. Buck would not stop clicking the shutter. His mind was racing and his hands were moving on their own.

Betty pushed herself to standing. "What the fuck," she said and kept saying it.

Buck pushed the shutter again, advanced the film again and again, and when he finally reached the end of the roll he found the shutter locked and the flash unresponsive. The darkness forced him to move and he fumbled his way back to the rear wall of the garage and slapped around until he finally landed on the light switch.

They just stood there in the new light. Looking to one another, then to the hole in the door. Betty reached for the croquet mallet and held it in both hands.

"How did you know that would work?" she said at last. "I mean damn I think you saved my life. That thing was… I mean damn. God damn. How did you know that would work?"

Buck was already back at the camera. Checking instinctively to make sure the lens cap was off. It was.

"How did I know what would work?" he said, now holding the camera as though it were some precious artifact. Something that may crumble to dust.

"The flash," Betty said. "How did you know it would scare that thing away."

He just stared at the camera. His hands were shaking. "I, uh…"

The fear on Betty's face turned to anger very quickly. Buck

didn't notice.

"You bastard," she said.

"What?"

"You absolute bastard."

She pointed the mallet toward him.

Buck held his hands out like he was trying to stop a car. The camera was slung around his shoulder.

"Hey you said I saved your life," he said.

"You just wanted a photo of it," Betty shouted. "It was after me and all you wanted was your damn photo!"

"They're your photos," he said. "Not mine, yours."

He shrugged the camera from his shoulder and handed it out to Betty.

"Your camera, your film, your setup. Your photos. And we just got something on there that I don't think anyone has ever seen. Something real. I mean Christ, I don't even know what I just saw, but it's on this film."

She looked at him a long moment then stepped forward and grabbed the camera. Her expression never softened. "What the hell was it?" she said.

Buck shook his head. "I don't know," he said. "But it sure as shit wasn't a hellhound."

IV

BIGFOOT

THE SUN was hours from rising when they came screeching toward *The Midnight Extra*. Buck drove the Volvo right onto the sidewalk in front of the building. He even forgot the keys in the ignition and ran back to get them so he could unlock the doors. Together they ran through reception and past the newsroom to the small cave of the photography office. The door to the photo lab was all the way in the back and Betty went through first and flipped on the lights.

"Stinks back here," Buck said, out of breath.

Betty surveyed the film processing room, stopping at the stainless sink and basin and holding the brown bottles of chemicals up to check the labels. "I like the smell," she said.

"Really?"

"It's familiar. My hands smell like it all the time."

Buck wrinkled his nose. He watched Betty grab a silver tank from a drying rack along with a metal wire spool before locking herself in a small closet. Buck kept asking her questions through the door. She told him to shut up. That she needed to concentrate. He waited less than a minute before knocking again.

"You gotta cool it," she said, her voice muffled.

"Thats an important roll of film."

"Like I don't know that."

The door handle turned and Betty emerged holding the silver developing tank. Buck stood in her way no matter which way she turned. "Have you ever processed film before?" she asked.

"No."

She thought for a moment. "Well I have to do this next part in absolute dark or else it will ruin the film," she said. "So you have to go."

"Really?"

"Yeah, lights off. You have to go."

Buck nodded. "I'll be right outside the door."

"No you won't. You're driving me crazy. I got this. Go write your story."

"Well yeah, but.."

Betty didn't wait for more. She pointed to the open door and then clicked off the light. When Buck was gone and the door was shut she flipped the light back on and processed the film in peace.

Buck went to his desk, sat down, then stood right back up. He circled the newsroom floor, then paced the hallway leading to circulation. Back and forth, there before the framed covers, the conquests of his younger self. The history there, the expectations. How the sad years from then to now suddenly felt as though they happened to someone else. A lost friend whose life you heard about on your way to someplace better and you pitied them a moment before forgetting them all over again.

"Hot damn," he said to himself. "Hot damn."

There was no way to celebrate but with a drink and he found several in his desk. And by the time he woke up, still warm with whiskey and wearing his clothes from the night before, he found the newsroom buzzing all around him. He rose and stumbled into the same small man who delivered the name of Mrs Vivet.

"Sammy!" Buck said. "Hot damn what a tip yesterday. What a tip!"

"Jesus Buck," Sammy said, looking him up and down. "You're a mess."

"Formerly," Buck said with a finger in the air. "A former mess. Admitted. Not today."

He straightened his jacket, only to find he wasn't wearing one, same with the tie.

"I may have gone a bit heavy in celebration."

"Buck you ran your car right up the sidewalk. Everyone had to walk around it to get in the building."

"Nope, that was for something different entirely. The drunk came later."

"You think thats gonna matter to Janet? Christ, give me your keys."

Buck turned out his pockets, then sat down heavily on his chair. Sammy took the keys, gave Buck a sorry look, then headed off to move the car. Faces peered over cubicle walls. Heads shaking. More sorry looks. A world filled with them.

"Just you wait," Buck said as his head hit the desk. "Just you wait."

* * *

BETTY POURED the chemicals with the steady hands of a surgeon. Developer, stop, fix, hypo, then rinse rinse rinse. She checked temperatures, referenced charts, and conjured up memories of having done this a hundred times before and why should this time be any different? There was the matter of a career-making image somewhere in that tank, sure, but film is film. She knew she slipped a few rungs on the reel, she always seemed to do that, but she realized it in time and unspooled it and spooled it again so the film wouldn't be touching against itself. Film touching on the reel meant ruined frames and god what if those were *the* frames.

She pushed it all aside. Rinse rinse rinse. The water cool and clear. But what if the developer was old? Or the fix? Old developer meant muddy negatives. Old fixer and you ruin them the second you pop the top off the tank and now it was time to pop the top off the tank and damn. Too late now. Only one thing to do, so she gripped the lid and pulled. The silver reel slid out and she took the end of the film and carefully, so carefully, began to unravel it. Photo-Flo for water spots, but that can wait. Not important now. Hold them to the light and come on, come on.

Water slid from the negatives and down her arms as she held them up to the fluorescent bulbs overhead. She squinted her eyes, pulling the negatives close, scanning them furiously from side to side.

*   *   *

WHEN BUCK finally opened his eyes he saw the familiar orange carpet of the breakroom. His jacket was draped over him like a blanket. His mouth tasted awful. He sat up and shook his head.

The breakroom sink was as dirty as the microwave but he didn't care as he leaned over it and splashed water on his face. It took a minute for the shame of the day to hit him, but when it did it was ferocious. He checked his watch. 4:00 pm. Damn.

Instinctively he looked for mouthwash near the breakroom sink. Of course it wasn't there. He settled on a pot of cold coffee. Good enough. He grabbed someone's mug from the drying rack and poured it full and took his first unsatisfying sip when he suddenly remembered the night before. It took that long. He only spilled half the coffee as he ran.

Betty was sitting behind a computer in the photography office. The overhead light was off and the room empty. Her camera bag sat neatly on the desk beside her, next to a light table scattered with negative sleeves and red grease pencils.

Buck tripped into the room and ran to her side, panting like a dog. She didn't turn to look at him. Her resumé was on the screen.

"What the hell are you doing?" Buck said, scanning the screen.

"The same thing you should be doing."

She clicked on the lamp beside her desk and tapped on a grainy black and white print laid out on the light table. It showed the floor of Mrs Vivets's garage, half of a misshapen shadow, and nothing else.

"What the hell is this?"

"That's our hellhound."

"Mutant," Buck said. "It's a horrible mutant."

"It's a shadow on the ground."

"No."

"Why do you think I let you sleep so long?"

He reached for a chair but there wasn't one so he dropped to his knees in front of the light table.

"No, no, no, no."

It was all he could say. The contact sheet was on the light table as well and he grabbed a small loupe and hunched over each tiny image, moving quickly from one to the next. The garage in stark contrast from the light of the flashes. Hard, dark shadows on the ground. The first photo perfectly framed, the way Betty set it up. Just a test shot. The next frame was when Buck must have grabbed the camera because all of a sudden it was pointing perfectly at the ground. Again and again. Just the ground. A single frame was circled with the grease pencil. The same frame Betty had printed. Half a shadow stretching over the floor. And that was all.

Buck was silent.

Betty clicked a few buttons on the keyboard.

Buck just sat there. He scratched his chin, feeling the stubble.

"I shouldn't have touched it," he said at last. "That's what happens when I touch things."

A quick knock on the edge of the door frame and Sammy poked his head into the office. "Hey Bucko," he said. "The boss wants to see you."

*   *   *

SHE SAT behind her desk with her hands politely folded. A single lipstick-coated cigarette burned away in the ashtray, sending up a thin stream of smoke to join the permanent cloud that hung above her. Buck wondered about that cloud. How many more years before weather patterns would begin forming inside. Little flashes of lighting. A downpour. Seemed appropriate.

She just sat there looking at him. He made to sit down but she snapped her fingers at him like a gunshot so he just stood.

"You know Buck," she started. "When I said the good old days I didn't mean college."

"Yeah, I…"

That snap again.

"Nope," she said. "You're just going to listen. I've tolerated decades of your madness thinking that maybe you still had some fuel left in your tank. Thinking that maybe you could come out the other side of this… funk. Whatever it is. But when I strolled past your car this morning on the sidewalk I started to have my doubts. Funny thats what it took. Imagine how I felt later when I saw you passed out in the breakroom wearing yesterday's clothes."

He held his hands up in surrender.

"I'm sure you have a good excuse. I heard you and Dorothea Lange there got quite a scoop so I'm going to chalk it all up to excitement. But look at me Buck. I'm not excited. Do I look excited? Am I sharing in the joy?"

He shook his head.

"It better be one hell of a story. A real blockbuster. Because in my eyes you've just gone from lazy to crazy and I'm not interested in getting on that ride. Understand?"

He nodded.

"Say it."

"I understand."

"You better."

She held up a photo that had been face down on her desk. A glossy black and white of an overweight and middle-aged Elvis walking past the Arc de Triomphe. One bejeweled hand was extended toward the camera, trying to block the shot, but the tenacious photographer managed to get just enough of the King's trademark smirk to prove it was him.

"Competition is stiff this month," Janet said.

Buck couldn't believe it. He broke his silence without thinking. "You sent Kip to Paris?" he cried.

"I did," she said, turning the photo to admire it. "And he delivered. Didn't he? This is what I want from my reporters. I mean just look at this. Real quality content. Front page shit. I may send him to Cairo next. Maybe Rome. Who wouldn't want to read about Elvis spotted around the world?"

She turned the photo again and slid it across the desk. "That's for you," she said, staring at him with her canine smile until he picked it up. "Memorize it. Burn it into your brain. Because if you can't beat Elvis in Paris you don't have a job. Got it? That's the high water mark. Your stunt this morning upped the ante. Now you're all-in. Hear me? Your adventures with your new friend better pay off. Now go."

The cloud of smoke pulled after him as he left, wafting into the hallway and following him halfway down the hall. When he got to the photography office he flipped on the lights without warning, interrupting Betty as she sent her resumé to the printer.

"We have work to do," he said.

* * *

BETTY WATCHED from the corner of the building as the last car left the lot. Her head was poked out from behind the red brick like a Hollywood spy and as soon as the lot was empty she signalled to Buck.

He was hiding behind the storeroom door, peeking out from a crack. At her signal he took a deep breath and emerged from the building.

Betty tried not to laugh. She really did. But the sight of Buck stepping out from the shadows of the storeroom wearing a full-body Bigfoot costume was just too much. It even had little feet. She doubled over. Laughing so hard that she went completely silent, making little gasps for air.

Buck was not amused.

"Alright, get it over with," he said. "We have work to do."

She took her time. Eventually she wiped the tears from her eyes and straightened herself while Buck stood with his furry arms folded across his rubber chest.

"Whew," she said at last. "Oh man Buck, this makes up for you almost getting me killed last night."

"Good, I'm glad we're even."

"Yeah, we're even. Now where's your mask?"

He turned back to the door and emerged with the Crocodile Boy mask held under his arm like an astronaut carrying a helmet and the sight of it sent Betty back into a fit of laughter.

"We're losing light," Buck said.

"Ok ok ok."

The Volvo sat in the center of the empty front lot. Buck stood in front of it a moment, rubbing his chin with a his rubber Bigfoot fingers, deep in thought.

"Alright," he said. "Get in."

Betty climbed into the driver's seat and closed the door. Buck stood outside the window and squeezed the Crocodile Boy mask over his head and then raised his hairy arms and hands in mock attack.

"How's that look?" he said.

Betty could only hear a jumbled string of words from inside the car. She rolled the window down. "What?"

Buck clawed at the air. "How's it look?" he said again.

Betty leaned back so her head was nearly on the center console and framed Buck as he pretended to menace the car. "You really think this will work?" she asked.

"Yeah why not?" Buck said, his voice muffled beneath the mask. "Horrible Mutant Attacks Area Drivers!"

Betty looked through the viewfinder and shook her head.

"People love a good car attack," Buck said. "How's it looking?"

"Well..."

"People love a good monster."

Betty snapped a few frames, but there was nothing good about any of them. "Maybe try growling?" she said.

"Growling?" The words came out as one syllable.

"Yeah, growl a little. Or roar. Something scary."

"It's a photo."

"Just try it. It'll be more authentic."

Buck tried his best mutant growl, and when that didn't seem to cut it he switched to a roar. Betty changed angles and fired off some more shots and they both got carried away just enough to not hear the car pulling up beside them. It idled a moment, then revved its engine.

Buck stopped roaring immediately. He jerked upright, peering through Crocodile Boy's nostril holes to see a man staring at him from behind the wheel of a pink Cadillac DeVille. A man who bore an extraordinary resemblance to an overweight and middle-aged Elvis. Right down to the mutton chops and sunglasses.

"Hey Bucko!" the man said as he turned the engine off.

The mask made a sucking sound as Buck squeezed it off his head. He wiped the sweat from his eyes with one giant paw. "Ah Christ," he said.

"Well ain't this a sight," the man said, heaving himself from the car. "Looks like I caught myself a Bigfoot!" He looked at the Crocodile Boy mask and shrugged. "Or a hairy merman or something."

"Mutant," Betty corrected as she climbed out of the passenger seat.

"Mutant, well of course." He held out his hand. Rings shining in the sun. "Kip Delancey."

"Betty Roy."

"Enchanté," he said, curling his lip. "You the new hire?"

"I am."

"And you got stuck with Harry Henderson here. What luck!"

"It's not so bad."

"No, I mean it. You're lucky. Old Bucko here gets to chase monsters while I have to listen to that damn Bearcat all day and night." He nodded to the Cadillac where a police scanner lay on the passenger seat. He shook his head. "Elvis sightings and crime reports. What a life."

"Looks like you got the Elvis bit down."

Kip smiled and did his best Elvis pose. Somewhere between stage magician and karate fighter. Head down and hands out with the fingers spread just so. It was pretty good.

"Well thank you little lady. Thank you very much."

"Wouldn't he be pretty old now though?"

"Sixty this January," Kip said. "But no one wants to see the king as an old man. No offense Buck."

Buck was slightly offended.

"I mean hell, I'm pushing the look as it is. I'm alright for Vegas Elvis, you know? But God help me if some young kid shows up here looking like he stepped right outta Jailhouse Rock. I'd be out of a job in no time."

"Elvis Discovers Time Machine," Buck said.

"Ah hell, wouldn't that just be the pits. I can see it now." He shook his head. "You just keep that to yourself Bucko. I don't need Janet getting any crazy ideas. She's so far up my ass right now I can taste her perfume. Called me about your story. Wouldn't stop going on about it. Telling me to sharpen up or my ass is grass. Figured she'd be happy with the Paris photo, but hey. C'est la vie, baby. Am I right?"

"Our story?"

"Yeah," Kip said. "Said you had a real scoop. I gotta admit this isn't exactly what I was expecting, but I'll be damned if you don't know how to commit. I heard those mutant growls even over the Stutz here. Ferocious! You're starting to look like the old Buck Vincent."

He turned to Betty. "You know Buck and I started nearly the

same time. I was doing crime reporting full time back then and Bucko here was the shining light of the Extra. He and Willie. They were like Batman and Robin. More covers than anyone."

"Willie?"

"Well yeah..." Kip said. He looked at Buck and saw the look on his face and his smile faded. "Ah hell that was so long ago it don't even matter. It's where we are today. Elvis and some Bigfoot mutant thing. Seems like things worked out pretty good."

Buck looked down at the rubber nipples on his chest. The tearing seams of matted fur and the tired old man beneath it. "Things couldn't be better," he said.

Kip slapped him on the shoulder. "Damn right," he said. "And I tell you what, this does look like some stiff competition right here. The old Buck Vincent is back and I gotta get to writing. Gotta shape up to stay in the fight. You two take her easy."

They watched him saunter into the building, whistling as he went. Buck couldn't make out the tune but he had a good idea who wrote it. He walked over to the hood of the Volvo and sat down. Betty joined him.

"Was he being serious?" she asked.

"I never know," Buck said. "Lucky son of a bitch."

The puzzled look on Betty's face stayed there longer than she intended. Buck didn't seem to notice. He was looking at the Crocodile Boy mask, then down to his furry legs and feet.

"This isn't working, is it?" he said at last.

"No," Betty said. "It's terrible."

He nodded, then just sat there watching the empty parking lot. The crumbling asphalt. A bleached soda bottle that rolled back and forth in the evening breeze. The sky now darkening and the vapor lamps flickering on one by one. "I'm too young to retire," he said at last.

"Are you?"

He thought for a moment.

"Yeah. Not by much, but yeah."

Betty nodded.

"You still have those smokes?"

She pulled out the pack and a lighter. Buck took one and so did she.

"You don't want to work here," he said.

"I need a job."

He gestured to the Bigfoot suit. "You want to end up like this?"

Betty considered the question, ridiculous as it was. Buck seemed to be in a mood. "No," she finally said, her voice serious. "I don't want to wear a Bigfoot suit. But I don't think thats the eventual outcome for everyone."

He was staring far out along the horizon, right to the highway.

"The suit isn't always as apparent," Buck said. "But it's there."

If he had a point Betty couldn't fathom what it was. He seemed convinced of it himself so she just nodded her head. "You can take it off," she offered. "It looks uncomfortable."

Buck just sat there.

A high cathedral broke above the treeline along a high ridge beyond the highway. Betty smoked her cigarette and watched the evening sun reflecting in a deep ruby red from a great stained glass window set below the building's spire. It held the image of a rose, but looked instead like a bloody eye watching them in the distance.

She had never noticed the building before, but now it was all she could see.

"What is that place?" she asked, pointing to the far hill.

"Brabane University."

"Looks spooky."

Buck shrugged. "Just some fancy school," he said. "I tried to get up there a hundred times for a photo of that place. Figured it would play well as a haunted castle or something. They ran me off every damn time. Security there is tight."

"Seems strange for a school."

"Yeah well maybe they just didn't want an old charlatan like me sullying their name."

Betty looked at Buck. The cigarette was slowly smouldering in his rubber bigfoot hand.

"Was Willie your old partner?" she asked.

Buck nodded. "Wilhelmina," he said quietly. "But she hated that name. Hated Mina too. Said she'd rather have a man's name."

"She's the one who dragged you up that mountain."

Buck didn't reply.

The evening sun dipped below the horizon and the red light left the cathedral window and the distant hills began to fade into the new dark. Betty lit another cigarette. "I lied to get this job, you know."

"Yeah I know."

"You know?"

"I saw your resumé. I was shocked to find out you've been working here a full year."

"Yeah well I figure a day and a half isn't going to look great for the next place."

She took a drag and blew out the smoke and watched it vanish.

"So where'd you really work before this?"

"The movie theater."

"At Hillside Mall?"

"Yup."

"So why try for a photography spot?"

"It's what I studied in school. It's like the only thing I ever really gave a shit about. And I'm good at it. I just didn't get very far."

"Why not?"

"I had to come home. Things were tight and I worked in that same theater when I was in High School, so I just went back. Thought it was easy money."

"And was it?"

"Well it was easy."

"But you hated it."

Betty nodded. "I was just so damn bored," she said. "And I came into a little bit of money in the worst possible way so when I didn't need it so bad I just quit. I decided to take a chance on something I actually wanted to do."

"You made more money at the movie theater?"

"One hundred percent more."

Buck just stared at her. "Janet isn't paying you?"

Betty shook her head. She finished her cigarette and flicked the butt into the parking lot. "I'm an intern."

"You're kidding me."

"Nope. Summer intern. Part time too, but I don't see the point in that."

"Damn."

"Yeah. So it would be nice if this worked out."

"You couldn't go back to the theater if all else fails?"

"I made kind of a scene when I left."

Buck laughed.

"Good for you," he said. "I hope you gave them hell."

Betty smiled. The night had settled around them and little clouds of insects sped around the orange glow of the security lights. She watched them a moment and thought of Mrs Vivet's garage. Buck must have been thinking the same thing. "We really did see something last night," he said.

"I know we did."

They heard the doors of *The Midnight Extra* open and close and turned to see Kip running towards them. He stopped just before reaching his car and stood a second with his hands on his knees, catching his breath. "Got something on the Bearcat," he said. "Traffic stops all night and then boom! Got us a wild animal attack."

Buck looked to Kip's Cadillac. "We didn't hear the scanner," he said.

"That one's turned off. Batteries don't last for shit. I got one at the desk in there. Got one next to my damn bed as well. Toilet too."

"Animal attack?" Betty asked.

Kip opened the door of the Cadillac and stood a moment with his arms resting on the window. "That's what they're saying. Ten ninety-one V. That's a vicious animal. They didn't call for an ambulance either. Called for the coroner. Got all sorts of units responding. They really send the cavalry when the suburbs get hit."

"Suburbs?"

"Some place called Cedar Ridge or Pine Glen or whatever the hell else."

He got in the car and slammed the door and started the engine. Buck hopped down from the Volvo's trunk and tapped on the window and Kip rolled it down.

"Spruce Valley?" Buck asked.

Kip snapped his fingers. "That's the one!" He reached over and clicked on the police scanner and the monotone voice of the dispatched called out for responding units and three cruisers sounded off in response. "Gotta be a hell of an attack," he said. "They've got the whole town in a stir."

He revved the car and put it in gear and skidded out of the parking lot and down the road and Buck watched him a moment before turning to get in the Volvo. Betty was already in the passenger seat.

V

CRIME SCENE

THEY SAW the police lights from a mile away. A chaos of blue and red that lit the neighborhood and the sky above it like a carnival. The knot in Buck's stomach tightened as they got closer. He knew which house the police would be buzzing around before he turned down the cul de sac. And when he finally did turn he saw the parade of squad cars and the growing crowd gathered along the street. The current of police moving in and out of Mrs Vivet's house, shaking their heads. Neighbors packed the sidewalk, whispering to each other in their evening slippers.

Buck kept his distance. He parked the Volvo at the end of a driveway three houses down and left the engine running.

"Turn around," Betty said.

"Not yet. We gotta find out what's going on."

"Yeah I know, but you have to turn around so we can watch through the rearview mirror. We're like sitting ducks out here."

"Watch through the rearview mirror?"

"Haven't you seen a cop show before? You never spy on people with the car pointing at them. You always turn it the other way and watch through the rearview mirror."

"Just get that big lens out."

"Amateur," Betty said as she unclicked her seatbelt. She spun around and turned on the lights above the back seat and started digging through her camera bag. Buck watched the house.

"This car is a mess you know."

"Yeah I know."

"I mean seriously. How long has it been since you cleaned it?"

Buck considered the question. "I couldn't say. It's been a long time."

"I found a hat back here."

"You'll find a lot of old things back there."

Betty plopped back down in her seat with the camera and the telephoto lens. She wore an old fedora on her head.

"What do you think?"

"I think it's a little big for you."

Betty flipped down the sun visor and looked at herself in the mirror. The hat came down just above her eyes. "It's like the Goodwill dumpster back there," she said.

She clicked the telephoto lens into place and brought the camera up to her eye and focussed the lens.

"Oh shit," she said.

"What?"

She handed the camera to Buck just as a gurney was being wheeled through the front door, heading toward a coroner's van waiting at the end of the driveway. No one seemed to be in a hurry.

"Mrs Vivet," Buck said, squinting through the lens. "It has to be."

"What do you think happened?"

Buck didn't answer. He scanned the yard and saw Kip standing among a group of cops, showing off his best Elvis poses as they laughed. Three squad cars sat in the driveway beside them. One unmarked cruiser was parked on the curb with what appeared to be an old Studebaker Champion in black right behind it. Buck lingered on this last car, unsure of why it would be parked among the police. He focussed back on the front door and saw a well-dressed woman emerge with a badge clipped to her belt. A detective, surely. The old man that followed her was as peculiar as the vintage car and Buck immediately placed them together. He was tall and lean, with brilliant white hair and round wire-framed glasses. His dark suit, so out of place among the police uniforms, seemed tailor-fit. He stood a minute speaking to the detective, then checked the time on a gold watch that glittered in the police lights.

"Friend of the family?" Buck muttered.

"What?"

"This guy talking to the police. Seems odd."

"Who, Kip?"

"No, someone else."

"Lemme see."

"Hang on a second."

"You've had it a lot longer than I did. Now let me see."

The man turned slowly and stared straight at Buck. Flashing lights reflecting from his glasses. He smiled.

"What the…"

"It's my damn camera Buck."

A face, huge and unfocussed, filled the frame. Pink lipstick and pearly white teeth. Hair set in curlers. Buck set the camera down to see the neighbor from the day before walking towards the Volvo in a pair of pink slippers. She waved her hands in the air.

"Mrs Turner," Betty said.

"Yup."

"See? You should have turned the car around."

She came up to the driver's side window and Buck rolled it down before she could tap on it. She took one look at Buck and raised an eyebrow.

"Well you have an unusual fashion sense, don't you Mr Vincent?"

Buck had forgotten about the Bigfoot costume.

"It's couture," Betty said from the passenger seat.

"Well I can see that," Mrs Turner said to Betty. "Very chic." She put her hands on her hips and looked back at the house and all the police cars and shook her head. "You know I'm very sorry about your cousin," she said to Betty. "I didn't have many nice things to say about her yesterday, but no one deserves to be mauled by a bear."

Buck turned to her at once. "A bear?"

"Well that's what they were saying. Can you believe it?"

"No, I can't," Buck said, feeling the goosebumps work their way down his arms.

"The poor thing was torn to pieces. The poor thing! I heard from Mrs Henry, thats Mrs Henry from two doors down and not Mrs Henry from the women's council of course, well she said… well…" Mrs Turner lowered her voice to a whisper and leaned in close. "She said parts of Mrs Vivet were… well… missing."

"Missing?"

"Like it… ate her," Mrs Turner whispered, mimicking a great chomping with her mouth.

She smiled nervously, then let out a little forced laugh, high pitched and cackling.

"Well thats what I heard anyway." She turned toward the house a moment, shaking her head. "It's no wonder a bear came sniffing around there with that yard looking the way it does. Probably felt right at home, like he's back in the jungle. And now he's on the loose! Can you believe it? A vicious bear running around our neighborhood. I've already thrown away all the honey in the pantry. I told the neighbors to do the same."

"Pop-Tarts too," Betty said, leaning over Buck. "Bears love Pop-Tarts."

"Is that right?" Mrs Turner said, her tone grave. "My goodness. All kinds?"

"All kinds."

Buck gave Betty a quick look then turned back to Mrs Turner. "Did anyone see the bear?"

"Why no, not that I'm aware of."

The Studebaker pulled away from the line of police cars and made the slow turn of the cul de sac. The windows were tinted black, but Buck felt eyes watching him the entire time.

Mrs Turner smiled and waved to the car as it passed.

"That well-dressed gentleman was asking the same question," She said, leaning back toward Buck. "I think he works for animal control."

"That seems right," Betty said.

"Well he was very interested in it. Very concerned. He asked everyone, but no one saw a thing."

Buck watched the car vanish into the neighborhood beyond.

"Did he give a name?"

"Why yes, I believe his name was Rathbone."

"Rathbone?"

"Yes. Mr Rathbone. It's a funny name which is how I remembered it. I've never known any Rathbones. Have you?"

"I haven't."

"Well he was very nice. Now if you'll excuse me I'm going to round up the kids and head home. This has been enough excitement for one night."

They watched her pluck three kids from the crowd and head down the sidewalk. A man walked reluctantly behind them. The police filtered in and out of the house and the crowd stayed and watched. Buck and Betty sat waiting in the car for what seemed like hours. Buck unzipped the Bigfoot costume and pulled the top down and bunched it on his lap. Betty leaned her seat back and tilted the fedora down over her eyes and slept. Buck just sat and watched the police as they finished their investigation.

Eventually the crowd began to dwindle. They broke off in twos and threes until no one was left but a few older kids. They seemed emboldened by their endurance of curiosity, edging closer to the squad cars, or trying to peer inside the rear windows of the coroner's van until they too grew bored and vanished into the night.

Kip squeezed into his Cadillac and started down the road. Buck reclined his seat and hid below the line of the window as he passed. No need to draw any attention. The dark coroner's van and the squad cars with their flashing lights all drove off soon after, leaving the street far darker than Buck was expecting. The Vivet house now stood quiet and alone in its wild yard, far back from the road. The darkness of it made Buck shiver.

He considered driving away. Strongly considered it. How easy it would be to just start the engine and drive right past that house and away from whatever horrors it held. Just so easy.

He nudged Betty on the shoulder instead. "Hey, wake up."

She stirred and looked at Buck from beneath the brim of the hat. "Time to go?" she said.

"Time to go."

She tossed the hat on the dashboard and straightened her seat-back. Buck turned the key and flipped on the headlights.

"Headlights?" Betty said. "Come on man."

Buck flipped them off. He put the car into gear and crept toward the drive.

"So what's the plan?"

"We get inside," Betty said. "And we see what happened."

"We do what?"

"We get inside."

Buck stopped the car.

"You want to break into a crime scene?"

"Well what did you want to do?"

"I don't know. I figured we could get some shots from the street."

"That was your plan yesterday. It sucked then too."

"We're not breaking in."

"Well we can't do anything just sitting here in the car can we? The story's inside."

Buck looked at the dark house looming at the back of the lot. The falling eave and the cluttered porch. He could just make out the letters taped to the storm door. "What if that thing is still in there?" he said.

"You saw all those cops. You think they could have missed it?"

Buck didn't answer. He rolled the car past the driveway and kept going.

"We can't just leave," Betty said.

"We're not leaving. If we pull into the driveway some neighbor's gonna see and call the cops. They're all on edge."

He stopped the car beside a row of tall hedges beyond the yard. He leaned forward against the steering wheel and peered out the window. "This is probably as good as we're gonna get," he said.

Betty nodded. "Do you have a hammer or something?"

"A hammer?"

"In case we need to smash a window."

"Jesus Betty, we're not going to smash any windows. We're going to peek inside of them and see what we can see. If you can get some photos then that's great. We're not breaking and entering. Got it?"

"Fine."

She turned and rummaged around in her camera bag and came back with a silver flashlight and a camera flash. She clicked the flashlight on and off to make sure it worked.

"That's convenient," Buck said.

"I always keep one in my bag. Helps find focus in the dark."

She switched the camera flash on and Buck watched as the little light on the back panel turned solid orange. Then she attached it to the metal shoe on top of the camera. "I'll keep my finger on the trigger," she said. "It really hated the flash last night. It might scare it off if we see see it again."

Buck considered her words.

"I really don't want to see it again," he said.

"You want your photo, don't you?"

Buck grunted a reply and took the keys from the ignition and stepped onto the pavement. He shed the rest of the Bigfoot costume and tossed it on the backseat beside the camera bag. Then he followed Betty as she crept along the hedgerow. Together they followed the contour of the sidewalk and then cut sharp across the edge of the yard. Betty hunched along and Buck followed close behind.

The light from the streetlamps fell off sharply as they made their way to the side of the house and soon there was only the cold moonlight to guide them. Betty slowed down, taking every step one at a time. Buck kept a steady hand against the house as he went. He felt the heat from the day radiating from the bricks. Betty stayed a few paces ahead and when they turned the corner she stopped at a set of shuttered windows and felt around the edges to see if she could pry them open.

"What are you doing?" Buck hissed.

"What's it look like?"

"It loos like a felony. Knock it off."

"I can't get a photo if the windows are blocked."

"There's other windows."

"Yeah but I can reach these," Betty whispered. "Besides, the curtains pulled in almost every room. I can get a look inside if I get this thing loose."

She got her fingers behind the frame and pulled hard on the shutter. When that didn't work she tried to pry the slats apart instead, bending them until the wood began to crack.

Buck couldn't watch. He felt his pulse racing and all he wanted was to go back to the car and then maybe head to the Crow's Nest for a beer. Forget all this madness. He backed away from Betty and felt the ground beneath his feet harden to concrete and realized he was on the rear patio. The concrete shined a dull white in the moonlight. Buck could see the patio doors and he walked to them and peered inside and saw that the curtains were pulled back just enough for a view of the dark dining room beyond.

Betty was still pulling at the slats on the window shutter when Buck called out to her. She walked over to him and cupped her hands to the glass and nodded.

"Hey, there we go," she said.

"You might even avoid jail time."

Betty stayed with her hands and face pressed to the glass. She looked around the dark house and shook her head. "I can't see a damn thing," she said.

"Nothing?"

"Well there's a dining table and some chairs, but nothing worth shooting."

Buck walked out to the edge of the patio to see more windows jutting out from the rear wall of the house. He started to walk to the first of them when he heard the sound of the patio door sliding in its track. He turned just in time to see Betty disappear inside the house.

He tripped on the edge of the concrete as he ran and caught himself on the glass-topped patio table to keep from falling. He called out to Betty with the loudest whisper he could muster and when she didn't answer he crept to the open door and leaned inside.

Betty stood beside the dining room table, scanning the room

with her flashlight.

"What the hell," Buck cried. "You jimmy the lock?"

"It was open."

"Christ."

"It's not breaking and entering if the door is open."

Buck thought a moment. "Is that true?"

"I think so."

Betty walked further into the house and there was nothing Buck could do but follow. He met her at the far end of the dining room. She shined her light along the top of a buffet cabinet, stopping on a framed photograph. She walked forward and picked it up and studied it in the light.

"Buck."

"Yeah?"

"Look at this."

He peered over her shoulder. The couple in the photograph sat on a park bench in autumn, holding one another. Her eyes were open and his were closed.

"That's her," Betty said.

"Who?"

"Mrs Vivet."

Buck looked again. The woman in the photo did not smile. You could see the affection in her eyes but it was of a serious nature. Something stong and fierce. Nothing at all like the woman they met. Her bottom lip was whole as well.

"It's like she's a different person," Buck said. He tapped on the man in the photograph. "That must be her husband."

He turned the photo over and read aloud the inscription

written along the back board of the frame: "Michelle and Steven, November 1992"

As if on cue, the sound of little bells tinkled in the dark of the house. Betty spun the light in their direction, but there was nothing to be seen.

"God those things creep me out," Buck said.

"Me too."

Betty set the photo back on the buffet. She started across the dining room with Buck following close behind. They crossed the entryway and Betty cupped her hand over the flashlight as they passed the windows of the front door. A faint orange light from the streetlamps came in through the windows and they used it to guide themselves along the entryway and to the threshold of the living room. Then they both stopped. You could smell the blood in the air. Like meat. Like a slaughterhouse.

Betty uncovered the light.

The living room was torn to pieces. Floorlamps shattered and fallen and the coffee table on its side. Thick streaks of blood on the carpet. More on the walls. A handprint too, shaped as though it was clawing away from whatever had found its way into the house.

"Jesus," Buck whispered.

Betty kept shining the light over the room. Neither wanted to take a step inside.

"Look," Betty said. "It must have come from the garage."

Buck nodded. You could see where the carnage began and where it ended.

"Get a photo," he whispered.

"Here?"

"Yeah here." He kept his voice low. "Make sure you get the blood on the walls. Over there by the kitchen, where it's heaviest. Maybe the carpet here too. And that handprint."

"What about the flash?"

Buck looked around the room. "The curtains are all drawn. Just do it quick. A couple frames and that's it."

Betty used the flashlight to find her focus then clicked the shutter. The flash popped, bathing the room in hard white light. Then again. From somewhere beyond the kitchen a bell jingled, then went silent. Then a heavy creaking of wood.

They froze. Neither dared to move.

"Did you hear that?" Betty whispered.

"Yeah."

"Probably just one of the Stevens. Right?"

"Right."

They waited in the darkness. Another bell rang out, but there was no other sound at all. Betty clicked on the flashlight and took a few uneasy steps toward the kitchen.

Dishes lay in shards all across the linoleum floor. A small wooden table, broken and upended, sat against the opposite wall. And there was so much blood. Everywhere. All the way to the ceiling.

Betty could hardly steady the camera. The flash popped once, then twice. Again the bells rang, deep in the house.

"Let's get the hell out of here," Betty whispered.

Buck didn't reply. He was looking at something in the shadows beyond the kitchen.

"Give me your flashlight," he said.

"No."

"Damn it Betty give me the flashlight."

He took it and crept forward, fixing the beam on the security panel in the hallway beside the family room. The keypad was covered in blood. He shined the light on the door beside the panel and saw that it was cracked open.

"Shit."

"What?"

"The basement," Buck said.

"She said they didn't have a basement."

"She also served us a plate of cookie photos."

The weight of the door surprised him. Like the door of a vault, gliding smooth and slow on its thick hinges. He shined the light into the dark as Betty peered inside.

"Well damn," she said.

Buck breathed a sigh of relief.

The room beyond was perfectly empty. Just a big closet. Betty slipped inside anyway, grabbing the flashlight from Buck's hand as she went.

"Goddamn it, Betty," he hissed.

"There's blood on the back wall."

"There's blood everywhere."

"Yeah but look, it's like she was grabbing at the edge."

"Who cares?" Buck said. "It's an empty room."

"Why would you have a security panel on an empty room?"

Buck looked over his shoulder into the dark house. "Drop it," he hissed. "Let's go."

"And look, there's something on the walls."

Buck leaned into the room. He saw Betty standing beside a

grid of small metal discs embedded in the side wall. She studied them a moment, then walked to the opposite wall and shined her light on a matching grid.

"They're little nozzles" she said.

"So?"

She went to the rear wall once more and traced its edges.

"This is a door..." she whispered to herself. Then louder: "Buck, this is a door."

He stepped forward into the room. "Don't open it," he said.

Betty ignored him. She looked back and forth from the nozzles to the rear wall, then without warning she walked to the door behind Buck and pulled it shut, sealing them in the room.

"What the hell are you doing?" Buck cried.

An array of tiny of red lights appeared in the ceiling above them, filling the room with crimson.

"Betty?"

"Just wait."

Another clicking sound, then a low hiss as compressed air filled the room from the metal nozzles in the walls.

"Betty!"

Buck could feel the pressure building in the air. His ears began to ache and he pressed his forefingers to them to try and stop the pain. Beside him, Betty casually pinched her nose and closed her mouth. Her cheeks swelled as she blew out.

The red light flashed once, then twice, then went out. The hissing stopped as well.

"It's an airlock," Betty said. "Right here in the house. How wild is that?"

Her words were muffled to Buck's ears, like she was underwater. The whole world felt like that. He took a minute to work his jaw and pressed his ears until the pressure equalized.

"You could have warned me," he said. "What the hell do you need an airlock for anyway?"

"For this," Betty said, as she pushed on the rear wall.

"Oh goddamn it," Buck said.

The hallway beyond was pitch black, but Betty's flashlight landed upon an electric panel near the entrance with three large red switches. She didn't hesitate. She flipped them on one at a time, ka-chunck, ka-chunck, ka-chunck, and a series of fluorescent lights lit up the hallway and the staircase beyond.

"Found the basement," Betty said.

"Shit," Buck said. "You're gonna say we need to go down there, aren't you?"

"Sure am."

Buck was silent a long time. He could smell disinfectant in the air, like a hospital.

"I don't think I can do that."

"We got lights now," Betty said. "You're just freaked out."

"I am definitely freaked out. You should be too."

"What kind of reporter are you? A hidden staircase behind a hidden door in a spooky house and you don't want to explore?"

"You know what kind of reporter I am."

"Yeah well, what would the old Buck Vincent do?"

Buck just shook his head. "You don't know what's down there."

"Our story is down there," Betty said. "And it's a hell of a story."

"It better be," Buck said.

VI

STEVENS

THE HOSPITAL smell only grew stronger as they descended. The lights seemed to get brighter as well, shining from the steel plated stairs and the white walls in such stark contrast to the house above it felt like they had left it behind entirely. As if it were a place they only imagined.

"Well you were right about the lights," Buck said, the whisper gone from his voice. "The lights help."

"Are you afraid of the dark, Buck?"

"I'm afraid of a lot of things."

Their shoes echoed off the steel steps as they went deeper beneath the house. Half a flight, then a small landing where the steps doubled-back, then a half flight more until the stairs ended at a reinforced steel door with heavy sliding locks and a porthole window. It reminded Buck of the kind of door you'd see on a walk-in freezer, or a patient's door at an asylum. Like in the movies where the lunatic jumps up to that porthole window and screams with his bloody mouth just as the handle is turned.

Betty must not have seen any of those movies. She pressed her face to the window without any hesitation.

"It looks like an operating room," she said.

"What?"

"Look."

She was right. Buck could see the operating table centered on the linoleum floor. It was surrounded by monitors and IV racks, all draped in wires and silicone tubes. Two surgical lights, their bulbs dark and cold, hung over the table like great silver eyes.

"For Christ's sake," Buck whispered.

"It's empty."

"You don't know that."

"I just looked," Betty said.

"Did you notice the curtain behind the bed?"

Betty looked through the window again, seeing the rubber curtain that she had mistaken for the rear wall of the room. Whatever lay beyond was dark and hidden.

She watched through the window for a long moment, then started flipping the latches on the door. "There's no one in there."

Buck knew better than to try and stop her. "Two minutes and we're out," he said.

Betty nodded. She gripped the handle with both hands and pulled the door open and stepped inside the room. Buck followed a few steps behind her.

They crept toward the operating table, avoiding the heavy electric cables that snaked along the floor.

"Look how big this thing is," Betty said.

Buck noticed it too. The operating table was a normal length, but wide enough to for two people side-by-side.

"Is that normal?"

Buck shook his head. It was certainly not normal.

A white linen sheet lay draped over the operating table and against Buck's better judgement he grabbed a corner of it and began to pull. As it fell to his feet it revealed a welded seam running the length of the steel table, marking exactly where the surface had been widened. It also exposed four leather shackles. Two along the bottom, and two along the top. They were bolted to the extended side of the table.

Buck took the pen from his inner pocket and used it to flip open one of the shackles. The leather was stretched and dark and the bolt that held the shackle to the table was bent to one side with the steel puckered and pulled up beneath it.

Betty walked to the foot of the table. "Are those…"

"Yeah."

"What the hell for?"

Buck said he didn't know. He looked over the monitors and equipment surrounding the bed, but made no sense of them. He turned to the rubber curtain and cupped his hands to its surface to try and peer through to the dark room beyond.

A heavy metallic crash, monstrous in the sterile silence, came from just beyond the rubber curtain. Buck jumped and let out a little yelp. Betty jerked her head toward the noise. They both froze and waited.

Silence. Then a tiny jingle.

"Goddamn Stevens," Buck said.

The fuzzy shape of a cat pawed its way to the other side of the curtain. They could see its contours distorted by the thick rubber as it went, stretching out of proportion as the curtain billowed, then reforming at the inward curl. Like it was reflecting in a fun-house mirror.

Buck started to laugh. Nervous and stilted at first, an expression of sheer relief, before turning into something real and contagious.

Betty just smiled and shook her head. "Creepy fucking things."

"I thought it was a monster," Buck said, wiping the tears from his eyes. "Thought we were done for."

The cat approached the edge of the curtain, close to where Buck leaned against the table. He bent down and held out his hand and made a little clicking sound with his tongue. "Must have gotten locked down here," he said.

The shape of the cat turned to Buck's voice. It walked closer to the edge of the curtain, still hidden, but coming into focus. It limped slightly as it approached.

"I think it's hurt," Buck said. "It's walking funny."

Betty hunched down to get a look.

"Don't scare it," Buck said. "You get some photos of the room and I'll try and shoo it out the door. Our two minutes is up."

"I thought you were afraid of cats," Betty said, standing up and turning back to the bed.

"I never said that."

Buck made more of the little clicking noises and got down to his knees and tapped at the floor with his fingernails. The cat stopped and took a few steps toward the sound. There was definitely something strange about its stride. Something out of balance that made the movements uneven. The rubber curtain made it nearly impossible to see, but it seemed to gallop with its front legs and hop with the back. Buck kept tapping his nails against the floor as he called and the cat ambled closer and rubbed its head against the rubber curtain.

Or were there two cats?

He bent down to see if there was enough gap beneath the curtain to see and was met by a pair of yellow eyes. The cat watched him a moment, then slid its head beneath the bottom edge of the curtain and reached out a single paw to swat at Buck's tapping fingers. The cat's second head followed right after the first.

Buck immediately fell backward, colliding with the base of the operating table. Betty turned to the sound and watched as the two-headed cat slid out from under the rubber curtain and casually hopped on top of the table. It watched her a moment with its four eyes, then began an oddly synchronized cleaning of its heads.

Buck scrambled to his feet. He backed into Betty and the two of them just stood there and watched.

Two heads. Perfectly feline, perfectly calm. Two sets of shoulders. Four front legs, two back. A single hairy tail like a lambswool duster that draped over the corner of the table. The cat licked two of its front paws while balancing on the other set, then ran them behind its ears and the sides of its faces. There was something hypnotizing about it. Spiderlike. Graceful and grotesque at the same time.

"That's a two-headed cat," Betty whispered.

"Get a photo," Buck hissed.

The left head turned toward his voice. The other continued its bath.

Betty stood still as a statue. The camera hung over her shoulder and she fidgeted around for it and grabbed it by the lens and was just about to raise it when something about the cat's motion stopped her. She saw a faint tremor in its body, beginning at the shoulders then moving down to the tip of its tail. At first the shiver was barely noticeable, just a twitch, but it grew more and more violent and soon the cat was shuddering uncontrollably.

Betty took a step backward. "Buck?" she said.

"Just get a photo!"

The fur bristled along its spines. Its claws extended and scratched against the steel table and it began to cry from both mouths. The sound was horrid. A twinned wail of pain and as the mouths screamed there came a sound like bones popping and skin stretching as the cat began to divide further. Like a cell splitting in two. Before the tremors, the twin cats were connected at the shoulder, but after, they were connected just above the hip. It shook itself like a wet dog and then began to nurse the new skin exposed during the divide. Pink and hairless and swollen.

"Betty, get a goddamn photo!"

Both heads turned to Buck and hissed. It made his skin crawl.

Betty brought the camera to her eye, but the cat scrambled beneath the curtain and vanished before she could she press the shutter.

Buck swore beneath his breath and grabbed the curtain where it met the wall and wrenched it open on its metal track, revealing the dark extent of the basement. It wasn't much. Just a desk in the corner stacked with television monitors, a row of metal cabinets against the far wall, and what looked like a clear glass incubator sitting on a rolling cart in the center of the room.

Electric cables ran in and out of the incubator like black snakes.

Betty stepped over them and tapped the glass chamber with her knuckle. "What is this?"

Buck shrugged. "Looks like a sandblaster," he said. "Or one of those plastic things they keep the preemie babies in at the ICU."

Betty found a small metal plate riveted into the metal just below the main glass panel. "Stasis Generator," she read aloud. "Model I3-F1."

Buck was on his knees again, looking under the cart. He saw nothing. "Yeah, well what the hell does that mean?" he said, groaning as he stood back up. "If it's not a two-headed cat I'm not interested." He turned to the desk with the television monitors in the back corner. "Only one place for the bastard to hide," he said. "I'll go flush it out. Have that camera ready."

Betty didn't reply. She was leaning over the glass chamber, trying to see inside. "This thing looks pretty serious," she said.

"Is it a big hairy cat with two heads?"

"No."

"Then it won't make the cover. Don't touch it."

Betty ran her hand around the back of the device and found a simple toggle switch. She flipped it.

Buck turned toward the noise. "What was that?" he said.

"Nothing."

The machine began to hum. Two small silver spheres, one on each end of the chamber, began to glow with a dull purple light. The rest of the chamber was empty.

"You touched it, didn't you?"

"Maybe."

Buck sighed. He was halfway to the desk, walking just as slow and silent as his legs allowed. When he got to the rolling chair he turned to call over his shoulder. "Ready?"

Betty's face was glowing purple from the electric light.

"*Betty.*"

She looked up to see Buck waving at her frantically, motioning that he was about to move the chair. He held his hands up to his face like he was holding an invisible camera. He made an exaggerated press of the shutter, then pointed at her.

"No shit," she whispered, but Buck wasn't satisfied until she had the Pentax held to her eye. She gave him an impatient thumbs-up.

"I'll count to three," he whispered.

Betty crouched down and framed her shot.

"One..."

Buck's hands pressed into the fabric of the chair. He could feel his pulse in his ears.

"Two..."

Betty turned the focus ring on the lens. She could see the chair and the cavity beneath the desk and...

"It's not there, Buck." she said as she stood back up.

"What?"

"I can see under the desk. The cat's not there."

"Oh for Christ's sake."

Betty slung her camera back over her shoulder and went back to staring inside the chamber. The purple light had coalesced into two flowing orbs.

Buck slid the chair out from the desk. "Where the hell did it go?" he said.

Betty found a dial on the side of the machine and began to

turn it. The purple light seemed to grow stronger and more focused as she did so. "Cats are sneaky," she said.

Buck sat down in the chair. He looked around the room and scratched his head then kicked his feet against the linoleum so the chair slid up to the desk. "For Christ's sake," he said again.

Two rows of stacked television monitors sat on the desk in front of him. They were small and square and he recognized them immediately as security monitors. He studied the wall behind the desk. Six cables ran up the corner of the room in a tight bundle. They each trailed off at the ceiling and he swiveled in his chair to follow one that ran along the exposed beams to a camera positioned directly above the operating table.

"Oh shit," he said. "I think we have something."

Betty didn't hear him. The purple light spanned out from both electrodes and stabilized in the center of the chamber until it was a single flowing beam of energy. The machine hummed softly. She could feel its vibrations in the floor.

Buck found the power switches to the security monitors and flipped them all on. The screens flickered white then faded to black and white scenes throughout the house and basement. Buck saw himself in one of the lower monitors. He waved his arms and his image on the screen waved a second later.

Of the six screens, three showed the basement. One above the operating table, one in the rear of the darkened lab, and one at the entrance, pointing toward the stairs. One camera in the house above pointed at the living room, one at the entryway, and one toward the drive. The images were still and ghostly in the infrared light.

Buck watched the living room feed for a long time. All that

blood, dark as oil. He shook his head and looked around the other monitors, noticing for the first time how a bundle of cables fell behind each one and ran in a thick bundle toward the nearest cabinet. He went to it and opened the doors. Six VCRs were stacked neatly on the bottom shelf.

"Hot damn," he said.

The purple light dimmed and turned almost translucent as Betty turned the dial. She could feel the vibrations growing, the electric hum amplifying until it was rhythmic and pulsating. She nearly pressed her face to the glass to see inside the chamber. How the beam rippled like water. That pale lavender color. As she watched, a tiny dust mote drifted lazy through the chamber, disturbed by the vibrations. She could see it in the pale light. It fell like a snowflake and then stopped as it touched the edge of the beam. It hung there, frozen.

Each VCR was labeled with a colored sticker, and when Buck turned to the security monitors he saw that they were labeled as well. The living room feed was marked with a blue sticker and Buck found the corresponding VCR and pressed play.

The VCR hummed to life and the live video cut out for a moment before it was replaced by a brighter image of the same room. A timestamp in the upper right corner read: AM 08:00 JUN 07 1994.

Buck checked the date on his watch and did the math. The recoding was a week old. "No murder on here," he said to himself. "Can't say I'm disappointed."

He hit the fast forward button and watched the activity of the living room as it sped through the day. An almost endless parade of hairy cats seemed to weave through the room as the hours passed. They ducked in and out of the curtains, slept on the sofas, and chased each other across the floor. The light slowly brightened toward midday. The window patches of sun traveled slowly across the room. At one point Mrs Vivet appeared on the camera holding a feather duster. She paced across the floor with a wide smile on her face, dusting nothing but the air. Back and forth, back and forth.

Something caught Buck's eye. He hit the pause button, studied the screen, then hit rewind and paused the tape again. A cat with a peculiar shaped head was caught mid-stride along the floral skirt of the couch.

"There you are," he said.

He pressed play. The cat crossed the room, stopping a moment to brush itself against Mrs Vivet's leg as it went. She waved her feather duster towards it lovingly.

Buck paused the VCR again. He cocked his head. Another one of the Stevens was draped over the back of the sofa, its three front legs caught in a beam of sunlight.

"What the hell…"

Betty found the opening on top of the chamber easily enough. It's not like it was hidden. It was just a little plastic door with a rubber gasket and a plastic latch. She popped it open with ease. She patted her pockets, but the only thing she found was her lens cap. Good enough. She held it above the open door and dropped it straight down into the chamber. It stopped as soon as it touched the edge of the energy beam, caught there in midair like it was held by a wire.

"Holy shit," she whispered. "Holy shit."

Buck scanned the rest of the tape. The footage speeding through the day until the datestamp hit 4:00 PM and the tape stopped with a thud and the screen switched back to the live image. The sun vanished and the furniture seemed to break itself upon the floor and the smiling shape of Mrs Vivet became a black stain of blood.

And there in the corner, a shape hunched over with its shoulders heaving up and down. Buck saw the stretched skin of its back. Just like he remembered from the night before. How it screeched in the dark. The flash of the camera and those teeth in just an instant and here it was sitting like an ape in the corner of the living room.

He got closer to the monitor. Inches away. And he could see how the thing's spine was splitting. He could see it plain as day. And as it sat there it raised its hairless head and Buck could see that the head was splitting as well. Two orbs of flesh, wrinkled at the twisted neck, and creased along the center. One smooth and human though it had a great violent hole above the base of the spine. The other gnarled and tumorous, twitching uncontrollably, like an insect. The monstrous head sniffed at the air a moment then dove down toward the creature's lap, pulling the human head along with it. Its shoulders began heaving again some unseen effort. Some struggle, or the end of some struggle, Buck couldn't say. It sat there a moment longer, then raised its heads and turned and began to crawl along the carpet. And Buck saw the creature's third arm for the first time.

The lens cap held there in the air and Betty watched it a moment and then began to turn the dial further. The humming sound intensified. The vibrations almost enough to shake the legs of the cart. A smell in the air like ozone and the lens cap twisted inside the

beam and began to lose its shape. It took Betty a moment to realize that it was melting. She didn't hear Buck calling her name. She
only watched the plastic ooze in midair and then burst into flames.
She tried dialing the power down, but the switch did nothing as it
was turned and the fire grew and the cart shook with the growing
vibrations. The light returned to its hazy purple, though now it was
ribboned in orange and in a moment it grew so bright that Betty
turned away from it and as she did so the chamber exploded and
all the lights in the room went out.

There was only darkness and silence and the smell of smoke.

And when the generator clicked on from somewhere above
them it triggered an array of red emergency lights in the ceiling.

Buck was already at Betty's side. She was on the ground and he
helped her get to her feet just as the security monitors blinked back
on, one by one. Buck looked at them and felt his stomach turn.
The living room was once again empty.

"Can you walk," he whispered.

"Yeah."

"Can you run?"

Betty just looked at him. "You saw it?"

Buck nodded.

"Show me."

They went to the monitors, each scanning the upstairs rooms.
As they watched, a large shadow began to crawl across the driveway
monitor. The Studebaker from earlier was pulling up to the garage
with its headlights off. It stopped just before the garage and the
driver got out and opened the rear door and once again Buck saw
the tall, old man with the stark white hair. He stood with his arms

folded, looking at the house.

A dark van with blacked-out windows pulled in behind the Studebaker and a small group of people emerged wearing white hazmat suits. Buck couldn't see the faces behind the masks, but there were four of them and they all stood in the driveway, listening to the old man as he spoke.

There was no audio in the feed, but by the man's gestures it was obvious he was issuing orders. He pointed to the house, and then drew a line downward with a finger to point at the basement.

"You ready?" Betty said.

Buck went to the cabinet with the VCRs and hit the eject button and took out the tape of the living room. He saw that there was a blue sticker on the tape as well. He thought a moment and looked to the other cabinets and saw the little colored stickers above the handles. He opened the nearest one and saw row upon row of VHS cassettes. Each marked with a date and time.

There came a thudding sound from upstairs, deep and heavy.

"They're breaking down the door!" Betty hissed.

Another thud. A crash.

"And there it goes. We need to leave right now."

Buck looked at the expanse of cabinets. He looked at the security monitors and found the one above the operating table. It was marked with an orange sticker.

"Orange," he said to himself as he ran along the cabinets. "Orange, orange, orange…"

When he found the cabinet he opened it and grabbed an armload of tapes and ran past Betty and headed for the door.

"You coming?" he shouted.

They raced up the stairs and into the airlock. Betty pulled the hidden door by its edge and heard it fall into place. The red lights in the ceiling clicked on and began to flash.

"Turn left and then sharp right," Betty said. "We're going out the back."

Buck nodded. He heard the hiss of the air nozzles and felt the pressure in the room begin to shift. His ears popped. Something brushed against his ankle and he looked down to see the two-headed cat weaving clumsily between his legs. He stepped away from it just as the red lights went out and the lock on the closet door released. Betty pushed the door open enough to peer out and the cat squeezed itself through the gap.

"Good riddance," Buck whispered.

Betty held up a hand. She waited a moment, listening. She could hear voices coming from the living room. "Ready?" she whispered.

"No."

She pushed the door fully open and stepped out into the hallway. Buck followed at her heels. There was just enough moonlight to guide her through the family room and out to the dining room beyond. She made her way as silent as she could and slid the patio door open just enough to slip through. It wasn't wide enough for Buck, but he didn't know it. His head and arm and shoulder made it through but his belly didn't and as he pushed on the edge of the door he could feel the floor shake behind him and as soon as he was through a cold hand grabbed him by the ankle.

It felt like a vice and he wanted to scream but something in him was actually too terrified even for that and instead he just turned to jelly, spilling out from the door like a marionette whose strings have been cut. The tapes flew out onto the patio, scattering.

Betty turned just as Buck hit the pavement. She saw the hand around his ankle and how it pulled him back into the house so she grabbed him just under the armpit and wrenched him out onto the patio. The hand pulled back, but Betty braced her feet against the house and managed to squeeze Buck entirely out of the dining room and into the night air but the hand would not let go and now here in the moonlight they both could see it and the arm that it was attached to. That long bony arm and that huge hand with nails thick and black, just starting to dig into the muscle of Buck's calf.

Another hand appeared from the dark cave of the house and gripped the edge of the doorframe. Then another. Two human hands prying open the door and that third one like a talon on Buck's leg and any moment the thing would appear in the darkness of the house and those mouths would scream in the moonlight and the thought was enough to make Betty reach for the sliding door and use all of her weight to close it. She felt the muscles in her side wrench tight. She heaved on the door, guiding it along its track like a guillotine until it slammed on those awful arms.

The thing cried out with its doubled voice. One high and piercing, one low and guttural. But it didn't let go.

Betty slammed the door a second time. Then a third. And finally the grip loosened just enough for Buck to slip away and roll himself to the edge of the patio. The arm slipped inside the darkness of the house and Betty could only just make out the glint from a cluster of pale eyes watching behind her own dim reflection. It screamed again and she turned and grabbed as many of the fallen cassettes as she could and ran to Buck and kicked him and told him to move his ass. He heaved himself up and ran. The streetlight guided them around the house and they reached the front lawn just as a loud crash sounded from the yard behind them, another scream, and they got to the car and Buck was speeding halfway down the cul de sac before they even closed the doors.

VII

VHS

THE ROAD was a blur. Street signs and stoplights and mailboxes and the dark shapes of trees flying by in the night. The orange glow of streetlights that lit their faces and left them in shadow as they passed. Appearing then disappearing. Buck gripped the wheel like a rally driver. Hands at ten and two, knuckles tight. His leg was throbbing and his pant leg was wet and he guessed it was blood and the thought made him press even harder on the gas.

Betty clutched the tapes to her chest with both arms. Only four remained. "Where are we going?" she said.

Buck shook his head. "I have no idea."

He drove like they were being chased. Downshifting into the turns then stomping the pedal. They hit a flat stretch and he floored it. There was nothing behind them but darkness.

"I think you saved my life," he said.

"Yeah I think I did too."

Further and further into the night. Buck sped through every red light he hit until finally he reached an intersection he couldn't ignore. He slowed the Volvo and stopped and he and Betty just sat there catching their breath. She rolled down her window and he did as well and the warm summer breeze flowed through the car. When the light turned green he kept pace with the traffic. His heart slowed down as well. His hands relaxed on the wheel.

They passed a shopping plaza and a car dealership and Betty recognized both of them. She told Buck to turn right at the intersection, then left and straight through the next two lights. He didn't ask why. A few more turns and soon they pulled into the parking lot of an old grey apartment building.

"What are we doing here?" Buck asked. "This isn't a great part of town."

Betty opened her door and stepped out of the car. "I live here," she said.

Buck swore under his breath and leaned forward in his seat to see the full height of the building. If it had ever been nice it was a long time ago. He turned the engine off and groaned as he pulled himself from the car, feeling the sting in his leg.

"Hey look," he said. "It's not a bad neighborhood. I just meant…"

Betty stood with the tapes in her arms, watching Buck struggle with an apology. He shut the car door and turned to face her. She just looked at him and shook her head. She started to laugh and tried to hold it in but couldn't.

"What?" Buck said.

"You pissed yourself."

Buck looked down to the dark circle around his crotch. "Ah damn," he said.

"How did you not know you pissed yourself?"

"Well a lot happened tonight Betty. My mind has been elsewhere."

"You didn't feel it?"

"I guess I didn't."

He looked hopelessly back to the car. "Well shit."

Betty turned for the stairs and gestured for him to follow. "For fuck's sake," she said. "Come on."

The building was no nicer inside than it was outside, but Buck kept his mouth shut about it. Half the lights were out in the hallway. The air was sour and dusty, like an old book.

Betty unlocked her door and turned the old brass knob. The apartment was dark and she disappeared inside and clicked on a wooden floor lamp and threw her keys into a little glass ashtray on a stand by the door. The place was small, but clean and cozy. Nothing about the building would have suggested it. Buck stepped inside and closed the door. He scanned the room, taking it all in. The wood paneling and the brown recliner. The puffy sofa coming loose at the seams and the leather-topped coffee table with its carved wooden coasters.

"This is your place?"

"Yeah, why?"

He looked at the taxidermied duck on the wall.

"No reason," he said.

Betty sat on the edge of the coffee table and unlaced her Doc Martens and left them by the door.

"Piss didn't reach your socks, did it?"

Buck wiggled his toes inside his shoes. They felt dry enough. "Nope," he said. "Stops at the knee."

Betty noticed the shredded fabric near Buck's calf for the first time. It was ringed in blood. "Damn, she said. "That thing really got you."

"Looks like it."

"How bad?"

"Well I'd say my pants are ruined."

"Yeah I'd say so," Betty said. "Wait here."

She vanished down a narrow hallway beside the kitchenette. Buck kept his feet on the entry mat. He felt like a dirty old dog that just showed up at the door. "Not too far off the mark," he said to himself.

"What?"

"Nothing."

Betty appeared from the hallway holding a pair of sweatpants, a towel, a washcloth, and a plastic grocery bag.

"Bathroom is at the end of the hall."

He left his shoes by the door and limped his way to the bathroom. His leg was throbbing. He undid his belt and winced as he slid the wet pants and underwear over his bloody leg. He tossed the clothes in the bathtub then held one of the washcloths beneath the faucet and used it to mop himself off. He wiped away the piss and all the blood and tossed the washcloth into the tub with his soiled clothes. What a goddamn night. He dried off with the towel then threw it in the tub as well. Then he propped his foot on the toilet and examined the five cuts along his calf. They looked about as good as they felt.

The cabinet behind the bathroom mirror was larger than Buck was expecting. It was the old kind, sunk deep into the wall with a little slit in the back for used razor blades. He found the rubbing alcohol on the lower shelf, next to the Pepto-Bismol and a bottle of cough syrup. A row of orange prescription bottles sat on the second shelf. Buck stopped a moment to think about that. There were more pill bottles than you'd expect for a twenty-something. He reached out to turn one of the bottles so he could read the label, then stopped himself. "None of your goddamn business," he grunted. He shut the mirror and balled some toilet paper in his hand and poured alcohol over it and dabbed it on the cuts.

It hurt more than he thought it would. He found himself stomping on the ground and yelling like a cowboy.

"You alright in there?"

"Swell."

"You need anything?"

Buck let out a deep breath. "I could use a beer," he said.

"Me too."

Betty's grey sweatpants were long enough, but the waistband was stretched to its limit. There was no need to tie the drawstrings, but he did it anyway. A full-length mirror was attached to the back of the bathroom door and Buck found himself staring at his strange reflection and just shaking his head. Sweatpants were not meant to be paired with a dress shirt and vest. His necktie seemed a little out of place as well. He went to the bathtub and stuffed the wet clothes and towels into the plastic grocery bag, hesitated a moment, then threw everything into the trash bin.

When he came back out to the living room he found a beer waiting for him on the coffee table. He fell into the couch and twisted the cap on the bottle.

"To dry pants," he said.

"And mutants."

"Dry pants and mutants."

They tapped the bottles together and drank. The TV was just a glowing blue screen. Three tapes sat on top of the VCR. The fourth was just an empty case. Betty held the remote with her finger resting on the play button. She didn't press it.

"I don't know if I'm ready to see it either," Buck said.

"What a night."

Buck laid back into the sofa and took a deep breath. Betty opened a window and lit a cigarette and gave one to Buck.

"How's your leg?"

Buck pulled up the sweatpants to show her the five jagged cuts along his calf.

"They hurt?"

"Yeah."

"You think you need stitches?"

"Probably."

Buck spread out his fingers. Even at their widest they couldn't reach all of the cuts. He shook his head.

"After all these years," he said. "An honest-to-God monster."

He rolled down his pant leg and took another drag of the cigarette. Another swig of beer. Somewhere in the streets below a dog began to bark.

"You think we're gonna see it on those tapes?"

Betty shrugged. "That's why you grabbed them, isn't it?"

"I grabbed them before I actually got much of a look at the thing," Buck said. "Now I don't know if I want to see it again. Certainly not sober."

He leaned back in the sofa and took another drink.

A photo of an old man in a yellow mesh trucker hat sat on the wall behind the TV. It was the only photo in the whole apartment as far as Buck could tell. Just an old man smiling in the sun. The hint of a river behind him. Buck tipped his beer toward the photo. "Your granddad?"

"Yeah."

"He looks nice."

"He was. This was his place."

She snubbed out her cigarette in a heavy glass ashtray beside the sofa. Suddenly all the furniture made sense. "Looks like he meant a lot to you."

"Yeah he did. He was like my dad. He raised me when my mom couldn't."

Buck took a slow drink of beer.

"Did you live here with him?"

"Off and on. Almost my whole life."

"And when did he… you know?"

"Die?"

"Yeah."

"About two months ago."

"Two months?"

She nodded.

"Jesus Betty I'm sorry."

"It's ok."

"Is that's why you left school?"

"Yeah. There wasn't anyone else to help out."

He looked at the photo again. The edge was torn and he wondered if there had once been another person in the frame. He decided not to ask. He took another long drink and wiped his mouth with the back of his hand. "He would have been proud of you tonight."

"Yeah? Why is that?"

"Because you saved a man's life."

Betty laughed.

"I mean it. You're a tough cookie. You fended off a mutant barehanded."

"Well the door helped."

"I might be dead if it wasn't for you."

He took another drink. Something about saying it out loud made it real. Betty sat in the brown recliner beside him and he looked at her and said it again.

Betty waved the words away. "Do you always get sappy when you drink?"

"Better than getting mean," Buck said.

Betty raised her beer in the air. "Amen," she said.

Buck raised his bottle right along with her and drank, then he nodded to the recliner. "Betty, I hate to tell you this, but that is an old man's chair if I've ever seen one."

"You must have one just like it."

Buck laughed.

Betty ran her hands along the worn fabric on the arms. "You know he subscribed to The Midnight Extra," she said. "That's how I knew about Crocodile Boy. He was a real fan. He was convinced that some of your monsters were real."

Buck looked at his leg. "Turns out he was right," he said. "Too goddamn real. And you know whats funny? Now that I've seen one I'd like to go back to when I hadn't. You'd think if you chase something your whole life you'd be happy to find it."

"I thought you said it was always bullshit. That you were never really looking."

"I was looking when I was young. When it was me and Willie. We chased all these things like they were something you could catch. Something real. We took it seriously. Well she did, at least. Most of the time I think I was just following her around. She was the real believer. Bigfoot and Nessie and little green men. Ghosts and aliens. She believed in everything. I was just along for the ride."

"Sounds like you guys were close."

Buck took a long drink of his beer. He tipped it all the way vertical and set the empty bottle down on the table. "We were married," he said.

"Oh."

"For eight good years. At least I remember them as being good."

Buck groaned as he stood, then he limped over to the refrigerator and pulled out two more beers.

"She died in nineteen seventy-five," he said, sitting back down. "Chasing a goddamn story. She drowned and died alone. And I wasn't there."

He twisted the cap off the new bottle and reached for the remote control.

"And that's about all I can say about it. Now are you ready to watch this monster movie with me or what?"

He reached for the remote and pressed play before Betty could say anything in response.

The cassette cicked and whirred as it spooled inside the VCR.

"I'm sorry," Betty said.

"There's nothing to be sorry for."

The screen flickered from blue to static and then to a black and white view of the operating table, seen from above. A woman lay on the table like she was asleep. Her arms laying flat at her sides, her head cocked. She wore a pair of white socks and a hospital gown up to her neck. Silicone tubes and twisted wires connected her to IV drips and a series of monitors that surrounded the bed on castored metal stands.

Betty leaned toward the screen.

"That's Mrs Vivet," she said.

Buck saw it too. She seemed so alien to the woman that served them empty cups of tea, but there was no mistaking it.

"What the hell?"

A man wearing a long white lab coat entered the frame. He carried a clipboard and a cup of coffee and walked with the casual confidence of a surgeon. He took a sip of the coffee and sat the cup on the foot of the bed beside Mrs Vivet's bare leg, then he walked to the monitors one by one, writing notes as he went.

"That's her husband," Betty said.

Buck nodded. He recognized the man from the photograph in the dining room.

The man left the frame for a moment then returned holding a small steel tray with a scalpel and a pair of surgical hooks and a dropper bottle of iodine. He rested the tray on the table near his wife's neck and then took the scalpel and positioned himself above her. His back was to the camera as he worked.

"The hell is he doing?" Buck said.

Betty just shook her head.

Whatever it was didn't take long. Dr Vivet took the instruments and left the frame once again. There was clearly blood on his hands.

They waited for him to return, but he never did. A small dark patch of blood began to darken the hospital gown, just below Mrs Vivet's throat.

"You think the bastard cut her?" Buck said.

"Looks like it."

"Why?"

They watched as shadows began to stretch across the floor. Dr Vivet reappeared, walking backward, motioning with his hands as though he were talking. A crowd appeared a moment later, following him into the room. There were no fewer than a dozen of them. All men and women, all looking like they were dressed for the opera. They nodded as Dr Vivet spoke. No one smiled. Buck turned up the volume on the TV as loud as it would go, but the recording had no sound.

Dr Vivet disappeared from the screen and then reappeared pushing the cart with the energy field generator. The video feed flickered with static as it got closer.

"There's your toy," Buck said.

Betty nodded, then leaned closer to the screen. "Look," she said. "There's something inside it."

Buck could see it too. There was something held inside the milky beam of light. Something coiled and living. "Like a worm or something," he said.

An old man in a black suit stepped away from the rest of the crowd and approached the stasis chamber. Buck recognized him immediately. "That's Rathbone," he said. "Son of a bitch."

The man took a pair of long metal forceps from the cart and opened the upper door on the chamber and slid them inside. They stopped at the top of the beam of light, but he turned the dial on the machine as he pressed down and eventually he had the forceps around the worm. He then turned the dial all the way off and pulled it from the chamber, writhing and squirming at the end of the tongs. You could see its strength by the way Rathbone held it. Like it could pry itself from his grip at any moment.

Dr Vivet produced a small syringe from the pocket of his lab coat. He took the cap from the needle and went to his sleeping wife and drew blood from her arm. Rathbone walked to him with the worm turning in the forceps. Mrs Vivet lay peacefully beneath them. Her lips slightly parted, her hair flowing around her face. The worm slipped and slid over itself, forcing Rathbone to hold the forceps with both hands to keep it steady as Dr Vivet took the syringe and injected it with his wife's blood. The reaction was immediate, and violent. It had been twisting itself around the ends of the forceps, but once injected it began whipping itself back and forth. Dr Vivet pulled the hospital gown from Mrs Vivet's neck, exposing a vertical slit cut just below her throat, held open by a pair of steel surgical hooks.

The worm found the hole with ease. It pulled itself inside Mrs Vivet's body just as Rathbone released his grip on the forceps. Dr Vivet took the surgical hooks from the edges of the cut and immediately began to stitch up the opening. He worked quickly. Once the last stitch was in place he snipped the ends of the thread and nodded to Rathbone. The crowd began to applaud.

Buck and Betty watched in silence as Rathbone addressed the crowd. He kept one hand on Dr Vivet's shoulder as he spoke. Dr Vivet only watched the body of his wife.

Soon the group vanished from the frame and Mrs Vivet was left alone on the operating table. Her body began to twitch, ever so slightly, and then she went still as a corpse.

Buck didn't know what to say. He held the remote and pressed the fast forward button and they watched as the timestamp raced though the hours until it hit 4:00 PM and the tape shut off.

Betty opened another beer.

"Not a bad idea," Buck said, pushing himself from the couch and walking to the kitchen. "Not a bad idea at all."

Betty went to the VCR and ejected the tape. She checked the date written on the label and compared it to the other tapes. "Next one is just a couple days later," she said.

"Oh good," Buck said. "Maybe he'll put a mouse in her this time."

The second tape began the way the first ended, with Mrs Vivet laying motionless on the operating table. The wound on her neck was a thin black line. Her head was turned and her hospital gown appeared to have been changed. Her socks now had little flowers on them.

Buck fast forwarded the tape until Dr Vivet appeared. He was alone, carrying a clipboard. As before, he went to each monitor and scratched down notes then he set the clipboard down and clicked the pen and put it back in his pocket. He stood over he body of his wife for a moment, hesitating, then he leaned down and gently held her head and turned it into the light. Buck saw for the first time just how swollen it was. One side seemed to bulge out at a bad angle, like something was growing from the temple.

Dr Vivet parted the hair on the side of her swollen head, exposing some shiny object that Buck couldn't place. He thought at first it was a piece of round glass, but then he saw it blink.

His stomach turned.

"Did you just see that?" Betty whispered.

It blinked again.

Dr Vivet reached into the pocket of his lab coat and pulled out a flashlight and shined it into the eye. He shook his head. He held his wife a long time, just looking at the eye, then he moved the flashlight back and forth, up and down. He jotted a few things on the clipboard and then worked his way down the side of her head and neck, looking closely at the skin.

He left the frame a moment and came back with a rolling chair which he placed just beside the operating table. He sat down in the chair and took his wife's hand and pressed it against his cheek and just sat there with his back to the camera.

Buck swallowed hard. He took a long drink of his beer and looked away.

The remote lay on the coffee table and Betty grabbed it and fast forwarded through the tape. Buck had his hand to his mouth and was shaking his head. "Goddamn," was all he managed to say. "I mean goddamn."

Dr Vivet jumped up suddenly and Betty hit the play button and they watched as Mrs Vivet's head began to gently shake on the operating table. Dr Vivet checked his wristwatch then grabbed the clipboard and began to write. The tremors grew and grew until Mrs Vivet's entire body began to convulse. Dr Vivet stepped back and watched, helpless. You could see the pain it caused him. He shook his head and turned away until finally the convulsions calmed and slowly stopped. He watched her for a long moment before holding her head once more and examining it in the light. It was easy to see how the growth had expanded. Now there was the hint of a nose as well.

"Holy shit," Betty said. "Just like the damn cat."

"That's impossible."

"You just saw it happen."

Dr Vivet vanished from the frame a second time. Betty waited a moment then fast forwarded again but the time stamp hit 4:00 pm and the tape came to an abrupt end. The room filled with blue light from the screen.

"Two more tapes," Betty said as she got up from the couch.

"What's the next one?"

Betty checked. "December twentieth," she said. "About two weeks after the one we just watched."

She held the tape out in front of her like it would bite. Buck took a drink and nodded. Betty loaded it and sat back down and lit another cigarette. She pressed play.

"Hold on to your hat," she said.

Once again the blue screen flickered to life. Mrs Vivet was motionless on the bed. The face growing from the side of her head was not.

It watched the surrounding room with wild rolling eyes. Its mouth gnashed at the air and screamed in turn and Buck was glad the camera recorded no sound. It screamed and screamed.

The neck below the face was nearly split from Mrs Vivet's neck, and the shoulder jutted out from just in front of Mrs Vivet's own. A protrusion that looked like the beginnings of an arm knotted out below the shoulder. All of it was thrashing.

"Good god," Betty whispered. "It looks just like her."

Buck hadn't noticed in his horror, but Betty was right. The thing growing from the sleeping body of Mrs Vivet was identical to her. "Jesus," he whispered. "That's not our monster."

Dr Vivet appeared on the screen. His lab coat was open at the waist. His face unshaven. Dark circles written clear beneath his eyes. He approached the second body, but kept a careful distance from it. When he reached out to adjust the new shackles on the bed Buck noticed the bite marks across his hands and wrists.

"I don't know if I can watch this anymore," he said.

As Buck spoke the body began to convulse once more. Dr Vivet looked alarmed by the speed of it. He checked his wrist watch. He was saying something, yelling maybe, and he backed away just as the arm split away from the body and reached out for his neck. He fell backward, knocking into one of the surgical lights as he did so. The sudden shift in the light made the thing on the bed even more sinister in shadow. Like something from a nightmare. It never stopped screaming. It's single hand bent like a claw and when it couldn't tear at Dr Vivet it reached for Mrs Vivet instead. It gouged at her face and neck, clawing and clawing. It took all of Dr Vivet's strength to pull it away and fasten it to the new leather shackle on the edge of the table.

He ran frantically off camera and when he returned he came

with gauze and bandages and went to Mrs Vivet and struggled to stop the bleeding. He bent over her sleeping body as the new Mrs Vivet screamed and fought against the shackle.

The last tape was only slightly better. The new body was now fully formed and nearly split, but instead of its violent thrashing it slept quietly on the bed beside Mrs Vivet. A series of tubes ran to its arms and Buck could see the whites of its lower teeth showing through a ragged, bloody hole in its bottom lip.

He pointed to the screen. "You see that?" he said. "Her lip, you see it?"

"Yeah I see it."

Dr Vivet appeared on the screen. He looked like he had aged about twenty years since the first tape. He checked over the IVs with such care it bordered on obsession and Buck could see his hands were shaking the entire time. By the end of the tape he had taken to sitting in the chair beside the table with his head in his hands.

The time stamp reached 12:00 AM and the tape clicked off and they just sat there on the couch in silence. Finally Betty stood up and flipped the switch on the TV.

"I'm glad you dropped the other tapes," Buck said.

"Me too."

He stared at the empty screen, seeing his own reflection in the dark bubbled glass.

"You really think that's who we met?"

"You saw her lip."

Buck nodded. Betty went to the VCR and ejected the tape and stacked it with the others.

"So then what the hell attacked us?"

Betty shook her head. "That's what we've got to figure out," she said. "If we go back to the house we can…"

"We're not going back."

"You didn't let me finish."

"We're not going back.

"We just need to wait," Betty said. "We can park further down the road and watch those people from a safe distance. We can follow them when they leave."

"Follow them?"

Betty went to the door and grabbed her boots. "I bet they're still there," she said. "They were doing containment or something. That'll take a while." She sat down on the edge of the couch and pulled the boots over her socks and laced them. "They might even be trying to catch that thing. Who the hell knows? We just need to get there. Now move your butt."

Buck didn't budge. He just sat and stared at the tapes above the television.

"The clock's ticking, Buck. We gotta go."

"Do you have a car?"

"No."

Buck nodded to himself. "Good," he said. "That's good."

He stood and walked to the television and grabbed the tapes.

"You know," Betty said. "If they're gone we can just head to the morgue or whatever and see if we can get some evidence of Mrs Vivet's body. She was grown in a goddamn lab so I'm sure there's something weird about her. If we could get like a tissue sample or something that could be real evidence. Maybe some hair. Simple."

"The medical examiner's office," Buck said.

"The what?"

"The body will get taken to the medical examiner's office. It's a government building downtown. And it's full of cops."

"Don't you know anyone there?"

"Of course not. Why would I?"

"Because you're a reporter. Don't you have like, you know, sources?"

Buck picked up his shoes from beside the door then sat on the edge of the coffee table to put them on. The tapes were in a pile beside him. "No Betty, I don't have sources at the medical examiner's office."

"Well we can talk our way in if we need to."

Buck took his time lacing his shoes. First one, then the other. He leaned forward and put his elbows on his knees and balled his hands together and pressed them to his chin.

Betty was pacing the floor.

"We can tell them she's a relative or something. Someone has to identify the body, right?"

"Yeah," Buck said. "Someone has to do that."

"Well it could be us. Or me. Whatever. We get in there and get a sample. But that's only if we miss them at the house."

She looked down at Buck and frowned. "We need to go."

Buck took a deep breath and got to his feet. He held the tapes under one arm.

"This isn't our fight," he said.

"What?"

"This isn't our fight. I don't know what the hell it is, but it's bigger than us. It's dangerous."

"There's a real story here, Buck. A big one."

"No there isn't," Buck said. "Not for us. Not for you."

He reached into his jacket pocket and got his car keys.

"Where are we going, then?"

"I'm going home," Buck said. "You aren't going anywhere."

Betty glared at him. She noticed the tapes under his arm for the first time.

Buck followed her eyes. "I'm burning them," he said. "We're done with this."

"Like hell you are."

"Like hell I am, now move."

Betty stood in front of the door with her arms folded across her chest.

"You're not taking the tapes."

"Move, Betty."

"You're not taking them."

"I'll tell you what I'm not going to do," Buck said. "I'm not going to stand here and let some kid tell me what to do. You've worked a real job for two whole days and now you're Perry Fucking Mason. I hate to tell you this, but you're not. This is some bad shit we've waded into and now we're in way over our heads. It's dangerous. You're gonna get yourself killed." He took a step to the door. "It ends right now."

"You're going to ruin this before we even have a chance to do something with it."

"There's nothing to do," Buck said. "It's over. We forget all about this and we stay safe."

"Aren't you tired of giving up?"

"What?"

"It's all you talk about. Haven't you had enough of it? You just keep surrendering. Like everything good is behind you and all that's ahead is shit you have to endure. Its depressing. It's fucking sad. And here is something big and you want to throw it away."

"You don't know a damn thing about me," Buck said. "You're just a college dropout who lied her way into a shitty deadend job. You think there's some great mission here? Some passionate calling? There isn't. You're not an intrepid reporter. You're just a naive kid with a nosering and no goddamn sense. You don't know anything. Now step aside."

She punched him without thinking. Right in the face.

He cried out and stumbled and fell over the coffee table backward, still holding the tapes. He lay on the floor for a moment, like he didn't understand what had happened.

Betty covered her mouth with her hands. Her eyes were huge. "Oh god I'm sorry."

Buck moaned out in pain. "I can't move," he said. "Oh god Betty I can't move."

Betty leaned down and grabbed Buck by the shoulder, but as her hands started to pull he screamed out again.

"My back," he cried. "Betty I think I felt it snap. Oh Jesus. I think you broke my goddamn back."

She let go and stood in the middle of the room with her hands at her mouth.

"Call 911," he managed to say. "Quick, quick!"

Betty shot up and ran to the kitchenette and grabbed the

phone from the wall and started to dial. It gave Buck just enough time to make a run for it. He jumped up and grabbed his shoes and sprinted down the hall and down the stairs and out the door before Betty even knew what to do. She just stood there with the phone in her hand, listening to the dial tone and Buck's tires squealing in the the parking lot.

"You son of a bitch," she said.

She looked to the coffee table and saw that the tapes were gone as well. Of course they were.

VIII

THE CROW'S NEST

BUCK CONSIDERED going straight home. He really did. But damn if he didn't need a drink after getting punched in the face. The night was young and the Crow's Nest wasn't too far away. So why the hell not.

There were plenty of open booths and Buck grabbed one just opposite the bar and laid the tapes down on the table in front of him and waited. An old episode of *The Twilight Zone* played on a little television mounted high in the far corner. He leaned his head against the high wooden wall of the booth and watched.

A worn out waitress walked up to the booth and took one look at Buck and shook her head. "Honey you look like hell," she said.

"Hey Linda."

"Hey yourself. I'm not even kidding. You seen your face?"

She reached into her apron and pulled out a set of silverware wrapped in a paper napkin and tore it open to get out the butter knife.

"Take a look if you don't believe me."

Buck took the knife and looked at his reflection. The sconce lamp on the wall beside him was just bright to make out the purple ring forming around his left eye.

"Well damn," he said.

"Honey that's a black eye."

"Sure is."

"You deserve it?"

Buck thought a moment. He looked at the tapes on the table. "Of course I didn't," he said.

"Well I hope that's the case. What'll it be?"

"Beer and a bump."

"I'll bring you some ice as well."

"I'd appreciate that."

Rod Serling was just breaking down the rules on the television. The volume was off and some awful song was playing on the jukebox but Buck knew what the man said. He could almost recite it himself. About the ground between light and shadow. The pit of man's fears. He would have tipped his beer to the television if he'd been holding one. Hell of a guy, Rod Serling. Hell of a guy.

A black plastic ashtray sat on the table with a pile of crumpled butts already inside. Buck called out to Linda and when she came back to the booth she tossed a pack of Camels on the table along with a pink lighter. Buck took one of the cigarettes and lit it. His eye was starting to throb and he touched at the skin above his cheek. It felt numb. He thought about what he said to Betty and felt bad until he remembered what she said to him. Then he felt better. He felt even better when his drinks arrived.

"On the house," Linda said, tossing him a sandwich bag full of ice.

"You're too kind."

He took the shot of whiskey in one gulp then chased it with a heavy drink of beer. A long drag on the cigarette and he just sat there a while with the ice numbing his eye. Shatner was on the screen, watching terrified from the window of the plane. Good episode. But when the monster appeared and was nothing but a man in a fuzzy suit it made Buck laugh out loud. Linda happened by the table and stopped to watch the screen.

"They're much scarier in person," Buck said.

"Well I should hope so."

"I mean it. Goddamn terrifying."

"Yeah, and what monster you see today? Another Bigfoot?"

"I saw a woman split in half on an operating table. The one half was asleep and other was insane. And I saw something with big teeth and two bald heads that I think was splitting as well. It grabbed my leg."

Linda just looked at him, but he was still staring at the screen. She saw the two empty glasses and told him to maybe take it easy.

"I'll take it straight," he said without looking. "Make it a double."

The rain was beating on the window of the plane. The creature stood on the wing, taunting Shatner between flashes of lightning. The other passengers looked at him like he was mad and the thing was only getting closer. "I see it," Buck said. "I believe you."

The whiskey came and Buck took a slow drink this time and leaned himself against the corner of the booth. His mind was just starting to form a welcome haze. Nothing like a good drunk to soften a bad memory. That house and all the blood. Just a story he heard a long time ago. It wasn't so bad. Funny even. Nothing to worry about. He looked at the tapes and thought about the different ways to destroy them and then he thought about just handing them to Janet instead. Might be enough horror there to get her off his back for a while. Maybe he could ride that wave all the way to retirement. Maybe he'd wait for the story to hit and then take a vacation. Somewhere out in the middle of nowhere. Somewhere far away.

He was thinking of small towns along the New England coast when a frail, elderly man with stark white hair and a dark suit came walking through the bar. He stopped a moment, then slid into the booth facing Buck. The wood groaned and creaked beneath his weight. It shouldn't have, but it did. The old man smiled.

"Hello Mr Vincent," he said.

It took Buck a long moment to react. He smiled because the man was smiling. He said hello because the man said hello, but there was something tugging at him and he remembered the Studebaker and the house and he started to push himself to standing.

The man placed a hand on Buck's shoulder. "Stay," he said, his voice warm and calm. "We have things to discuss."

Buck pulled away, but stayed in the booth. The man unbuttoned his black herringbone jacket and smoothed out the fabric of his vest. He took his glasses off and checked the lenses against the lamp and took out a pocket square from his vest and began to clean them. Buck just sat there and stared. An ivory lock of hair fell over the man's lowered face and he casually brushed it back behind his ear. There was something youthful about the gesture. A kind of casual grace. He checked the lenses once more, then put them on and extended a thin hand across the table. Veins snaking over the bones. Skin like paper. Gold rings and a gold watch.

Buck took the man's hand and shook it. The strength of the old man's grip surprised him.

"Godfrey Rathbone," the man said. "It's a pleasure."

Buck took a drink of his whiskey.

"I know," he said. "Hell of a name."

Rathbone smiled. "It's awful, isn't it? I don't think it matches the man. How tragic when the inner and the outer are mismatched. Do you ever feel that?"

"Can't say I do."

"I find myself plagued by it. Sometimes I barely recognize my own face. This old man. Where did he come from? It certainly isn't what's inside."

Buck shrugged, unsure of what to say. He looked to the television and took another drink. Shatner was screaming.

"Well it's whats inside that counts," he said at last.

Rathbone grinned.

"Do you always speak in platitudes Mr Vincent?"

"I'm in a thoughtful mood."

"It would seem so. I only thought that you might share in this observation. You seem to be a man in conflict."

"Is that how I seem?"

Rathbone gestured to the tapes sitting on the table. "Would you have stolen those a week ago? Would you have even cared? Was the man creeping through Dr Vivet's basement the same one that wrote about hellhounds in last Sunday's paper?"

Buck looked at Rathbone then looked away. There was something in the man's eyes he didn't like. A coldness that didn't jive with the warm smile. He reached out to the pack of cigarettes and pushed them toward Rathbone who waved them away.

"You're gonna smell like them anyway," Buck said. "Might as well."

"I never developed a taste," Rathbone said. "They've always seemed a strange habit to me. Suicide for cowards. I've never known a truly happy person to partake."

Buck looked at the cigarette between his own fingers. He wanted to argue, but couldn't.

"Why don't you just tell me what the hell you want," he said.

"I want to talk. That's all."

"That's all?"

Rathbone held out his arm and gestured to the bar. "Whatever malice you think I'm capable of certainly wouldn't play out in a place like this, would it?" He leaned in close and whispered: "Too many witnesses."

Buck felt his hands go numb. Whatever frightened expression came across his face was enough to make Rathbone lean back in the booth and laugh.

"Oh Mr Vincent, you have me all wrong."

"I saw the tapes," Buck managed to say.

Rathbone turned the tapes on the table and read the dates printed along the spines. He thought a moment, tapping his fingers on the table, then nodded. "You got quite the show, didn't you?"

Buck didn't say anything at all. His mouth felt dry and he reached for the whiskey.

"Tell me," Rathbone said. What did you make of Doctor Vivet?"

The whiskey tasted familiar and warm. A few more and Buck

felt he might make it through the whole conversation. "I'd say he was in over his head."

Rathbone laughed again. He slapped the table. Buck jumped in his seat. He went to take another drink of the whiskey, but found it was already gone. Shatner was being forced to swallow a pill on the television.

"In over his head," Rathbone exclaimed. "Yes I would have to agree with you there. He is most certainly in over his head. I'm sure you can relate."

Linda walked to the table with another whiskey and another beer. "Read your mind," she said with a wink. She turned to Rathbone and looked him up and down, examining him like he was from another planet. "You having the same?"

"Rye Manhattan. Up."

She rolled her eyes and left, muttering to herself. Rathbone watched her go.

"The poor doctor," he said, turning back to Buck. "A lost soul. But that was a tragedy of his own design. Tell me, Mr Vincent, have you ever been in love?"

Buck said nothing.

"It is a terrible thing. It makes men lose their minds. Brilliant men, stupid men, it makes no difference. Love is a great equalizer. Wouldn't you agree?"

The whiskey was filled so high it nearly crested the rim of the glass. It ran over Buck's fingers as he raised it. "Love conquers all," he said as he drank.

Rathbone smiled.

"Another platitude, but my how appropriate. Love conquers

and consumes. It truly does. And when that love was gone the poor doctor did everything he could to get it back. Wouldn't you?"

Buck looked at Rathbone a long moment then downed the last of his whiskey and wiped his mouth with the back of hand then waved to Linda. "Dead is dead," he said at last.

"I could argue with that," Rathbone said. "But in this case it is irrelevant. Michelle was very much alive when we performed the implant."

"Is that what you're calling it? Cutting her open for that worm thing?"

"You do it a great disservice to call it a worm. It's more like a set of cellular instructions. A regenerative catalyst."

"Looked a lot like a big worm to me."

"It's appearance is irrelevant. It's method of reproduction is what matters."

Buck felt the room just beginning to dance. He felt a little smile at the edge of lips and knew it had nothing to do with the conversation or the night or anything else. It had one source and he looked at the glass in front of him and found it empty again. He looked for Linda. Rathbone kept talking. More nonsense. Whatever fear he had of the man seemed to be evaporating. Shatner eyed a police officer's gun on the screen.

"The cat was a great success" Rathbone said. "It gave the doctor hope. He pleaded to accelerate to human testing and I allowed it. But you saw what that yielded, didn't you? You saw it on the tapes. That hollow thing sprouting from her side. It looked the part, but there was nothing inside." He tapped a bony finger to his chest, right above the heart. "It was never any trouble for the cats, but my god what it did to a human. My god."

Buck's mind was drifting lazy from one thought to the next. A dozen goddamn cats. The doctor holding his wife's hand in that cold silent room. Teeth in the dark.

"The hell are you telling me all this?" he muttered.

"Because you need to know what hunts you," Rathbone said.

"It wasn't her that grabbed my leg," Buck said, slurring the words lightly together. "Sure as hell wasn't her."

"No, it certainly wasn't."

"So then spill it."

"The experiment was a complete success, it is important to remember that. Mrs Vivet's blood was alive and thriving during the transplant. The gestation advanced exactly as expected. But it didn't matter. You saw the surrogate's development on these tapes. You saw it screaming and tearing at the world. What you didn't see was how it managed to claw out the throat of the real Mrs Vivet while she lay on that operating table. How it killed her without hesitating. No one anticipated that. It raised the most alarming questions. She was a perfect cellular match, but there was something missing. Something fundamental. I decided to try and tame that awful creature, hoping to understand it, to mold it into the doctor's dead wife. Anything to sooth his troubled mind."

Rathbone thought a moment and shook his head.

"It didn't work," he said. "The doctor folded in on himself. He was a broken man. An absolute genius, but mad with despair. He became convinced that the vessel was the problem. That his wife's mind was gone and the resulting birth was broken because of it. His solution was to perform the procedure on himself. He believed his memory and love would be enough. That she could return to him. Do you understand?"

Buck was having trouble focussing his eyes. Linda walked by and slid another whiskey in front of him and set the Manhattan in front of Rathbone. The thin martini glass looked out of place on the table as Rathbone did in the bar. Buck smiled at this and took up his whiskey and raised it in a toast and drank.

"What did you ask me?" he said.

"Do you understand what I've told you?"

Buck smiled at Rathbone and nodded. "Not a goddamn word."

Shatner made a move for the police officer's gun. Attaboy Will. Show 'em who's boss.

Rathbone leaned forward.

"You need to listen to me, Mr Vincent," he said. "Michelle was dead when the doctor drew her blood the second time."

"Well that's a shame."

"Look at me."

Buck rocked his head from the television to Rathbone.

"The blood of the living created an abomination."

Buck nodded.

"So then what would the blood of the dead create?"

Buck looked down and saw the cold butt of his cigarette between his fingers. He dropped it into the ashtray and fumbled a new one out of the pack and lit it.

Shatner eyed the emergency exit. He buckled himself in and cracked it open.

"I'd say it would look like a skinned ape," Buck said. "It'd have a twitching head and sharp claws and it would grab me by the leg.

How's that? I'd say it would be a real goddamn monster. And I'd say it's your problem and not mine and you can take these goddamn tapes and get the hell out of here and forget all about me. I know I'm planning to do the same. You're telling me all this like I care to know it. I don't." He tapped the whiskey glass with his fingernail. "And a few more of these and I ought to forget you were even here. That's my plan at least."

"You can't just forget about this, Mr Vincent."

Another drink.

"Watch me."

"It's tasted your blood."

"Well I hope it likes bourbon and Schlitz."

"It's hunting you. Do you understand that?"

The plane landed and they carted Shatner away, raving and mad. No justice at all.

Rathbone took a business card from his inner pocket and set it on the table.

"I can help, Mr Vincent. It would be foolish of you to ignore that. For Betty's sake if not for your own. She's in quite over her head as well."

Buck turned from the television and looked Rathbone square in the eyes. "What makes you think I give a damn?" he said.

Rathbone tapped the business card and straightened his jacket as he stood. He checked the time on his watch then leaned over and took the VHS tapes.

Linda came with another whiskey, passing Rathbone in the aisle as he left. He stopped her and bent down to speak into her ear. She looked taken aback. She shook her head and Rathbone put a hand on her shoulder and smiled and handed her something that Buck couldn't see. She looked at it a long moment, then put it in her pocket and shrugged. Rathbone walked to the bartender as Linda got to the booth.

"Some friend you got there," she said.

"What did he want?"

She hesitated, then smiled and handed Buck his drink. "Just wanted to pay your tab."

"What a gentleman."

"You want another bag of ice? That eye is looking meaner and meaner."

"I'd love one."

She turned and left and Buck saw that Rathbone was gone as well. Good riddance. He looked at the untouched Manhattan and took it by the stem and bought it to his lips.

"Well damn," he said. "That's not half bad."

He turned to the bar and raised the glass. "Not half bad!" he called.

The bartender nodded. Two guys at the bar raised their glasses in solidarity.

Buck took another drink and thought of Betty's fist and Rathbone's awful smile and every other terrible thing that had happened in the day. Too many to count. Betrayal and lies with Buck at the receiving end. Fuck 'em. Why listen to a madman. Why care for anyone at all. He tore the business card into pieces without even bothering to read it. He let the pieces fall into the ashtray then tipped the Manhattan back and swallowed it like it was water. He lit another cigarette and reached for the whiskey. Another episode of *The Twilight Zone* came on and there was Rod Serling again. Looking sharp as a tack. That knowing grin. Stone dead at fifty. The pit of all man's fears and all the rest of it. A door in outer space and the ghosts of another life. Up past bedtime. The flicker of the screen. Thick carpet and the wood paneled walls and Dad smoking in the study. Always the smell of smoke. Mom at the sink. Both so long gone. Another life, another life. Dark water and waves. A sinking skiff. The cold, cold undertow. No idea what it stole. No idea at all. Watching in bed together with her head on his shoulder. Smell of roses. How warm she was. Another drink and before Rod even left the screen the Crow's Nest seemed to be falling in whatever direction Buck pointed his eyes. He felt sick and knew he would be sick and thought that maybe just leaning his head back would keep it at bay. He found the corner of the booth and collapsed there, feeling terrified and very, very alone.

IX

AUTOPSY

BETTY WOKE before the dawn. She sat shivering on the edge of her bed with her toes barely touching the rugless floor. Rings of sweat marked her shirt. The world beyond her bedroom window seemed frozen in the halflight. Oak trees and power lines and the far dark outline of a neighboring building caught in the dim morning fog. The utter stillness of it. Not even the birds were awake.

When she got to the bathroom she could feel the throbbing in her hand and in the vanity light she could see how the knuckles were swollen and bruised. She thought of Buck and wondered how his face must look and then realized she didn't care. Bastard. Two aspirin and forget about it.

She made a pot of coffee and poured a mug and sat on the couch. She turned the television on and muted the sound. It was barely worth watching now anyway. Infomercials and little else. The Thighmaster, the Kitchen Wizard. Four easy payments. Smiles and smiles.

In her dream she lay on the same table as Mrs Vivet. Bound hands and feet. Surgical lights and monitors and the glass eye of the camera watching her from the rafters. Needles and tubes. The tearing at her side.

She turned the television off and looked at her reflection in the dark glass. Then she looked at the face of her grandfather smiling in the sun. That photo there reminding her of her own loneliness, but taking it down would only twist the knife. You would have made him proud, Buck said. As if it mattered. As if some good can come from impressing the dead. She would rather have him alive and disappointed. The status quo.

In the end, it wasn't sadness that compelled her to get dressed. It was anger. There wasn't anyone left to prove herself to and she felt it with some razor clarity that hadn't been there the day before. Months of crying, of despair, and finally she found some fucking purpose and it had been taken away when Buck left with those goddamn tapes. And now she was alone and she could feel herself drifting again and there wasn't anyone left alive that cared. No one left to help. Just like before. The thought made her ball her hands into fists. Fine. So be it. She had better things to do than cry.

She pulled on her jeans and a pair of mismatched socks and an old black shirt. Her Doc Martens were beside the door and she sat in the brown recliner while she laced them. She found her camera bag beside the couch and checked to make sure the front pocket was full of film. Then she slung the bag over her shoulder and left.

The morning air was cool, but pleasant. The bus stop was four blocks away and she sat alone on the cold wooden bench and read the graffiti sprayed along the sidewalk and the municipal trash can. The bus came a few minutes later and she paid her fare and took a window seat and watched the grey world turn bright. The streets and sidewalks began to fill with people. The bus as well. They crested a hill and the early sunlight fell through the dusty bus window and touched her face.

A middle aged man saw her as he passed and told her she should smile. An elderly woman asked her what was wrong. She ignored them both. The camera bag was on her lap and the disc-man spinning inside the front pocket and PJ Harvey was telling some unlucky someone that she was going to twist their head off.

The bus wheeled into the downtown station and she got out and watched it roll away. The sun was only halfway down the tallest buildings and by the time she reached the county medical exam-iner's office it had reached the sidewalk.

The building was uninviting, even for a government office. Just grey concrete and tinted windows. Nothing green in sight. Betty walked through the empty parking lot and up the stairs and tried the front door. It didn't budge. She cupped her hands to the glass and looked inside. A waiting room, a front desk, and no one behind it. She checked her watch and sighed.

Around back she found three sets of garage doors and in the distance an older woman standing alone on a concrete landing just beyond an emergency exit. You could see how short she was in relation to the door behind her. She almost had to reach up to lean against the pipe railing. The morning sun fell on her face and she stood in its light watching nothing in the distance, but watching it intently. The door behind her was propped open with a brick.

Betty kept to the corner of the building and stayed out of the woman's sight. She hunched down behind a grey stone wall sepa-rating the garage bays and waited. She tried to gauge the distance to the concrete landing. Fifty feet, give or take. Doable. She slipped the camera bag from her shoulder and checked to see if the straps were tight. Then she scoured the ground around her until she found an old McDonald's bag filled with old napkins and ketchup packets which she bunched up into a tight ball.

The woman continued to watch the quiet world around her. She closed her eyes and took a deep breath and turned to go back inside. Instead of opening the door she stood in front of it and waited. As though she had to prepare herself for something within the building. As though there were some event unfolding or about to unfold that she wanted no part of but was caught within regardless. Betty could see the hesitation. Clear as day.

Finally the woman grabbed the edge of the emergency exit and pulled it open and vanished.

Betty sprang to life. She scrambled out from behind the wall and ran the fifty feet to the landing and jumped the bottom steps and held the McDonald's bag out in front of her and aimed it at the closing gap in the door. To her amazement it actually worked. The bag crumpled, but kept the door from latching shut. She stood up and pumped her fist in the air. Her heart was pounding. She took a deep breath and climbed the last two stairs and pulled the door open and kicked away the McDonald's bag and slipped inside.

The woman just stood there in the hall watching her.

"Really?" she said.

A series of bad ideas ran through Betty's mind. She picked the best of them and held out her hand and smiled. "Good morning," she said.

The woman just stood there. "Are you lost?" she asked.

"Well. No, I guess. Not really."

"High?"

"No. Of course not."

"So you're not lost, and you're not high, but you did just try and break into the county medical examiner's office at seven in the morning."

Betty just stood there.

"Are you going to tell me why?"

"The front door was locked."

"Was it?"

"Yeah."

"Well that's probably because it's seven in the morning. We tend to lock our doors while we're closed. Inconvenient, I know."

"Right, but I needed to get inside."

"Clearly. And now you're inside."

"Here I am."

The woman kept her arms folded, waiting for Betty to speak.

Betty thought for a moment, but only a brief one. She was actually prepared. "It's my aunt," she sputtered. "She was brought here last night."

The woman's expression softened, but only slightly. "Your aunt."

"Yeah."

"And did someone call you down to identify?"

Betty nodded.

The woman seemed to relax. "Well I'm sorry for your loss," she said. "I really am. But the front office opens at nine and not seven. There's nothing I can do before then. They have paperwork you'll need to fill out and everything else. It's really not my department." She made a sweeping motion with her hands, trying to usher Betty back through the emergency exit. "If you come back later they'll take care of you, ok? And for Christ's sake go through the front door."

Betty stood her ground. "I really need to do it now," she said. "My mom's sick and needs her medicine by eight thirty. I took the bus down early hoping someone could help me out."

"Well I'm not sure what to tell you."

"Can't you just let me see the body? I mean, identify it."

"No, I can't."

Betty tried to muster some tears. "My mom really needs me to do this. She couldn't come herself. Aunt Michelle and her were so close…"

The woman's face changed.

"Aunt Michelle?"

Betty nodded.

"What was her last name?"

"Vivet."

The woman looked at Betty a long time. Longer than anyone would be comfortable with. Thirty seconds. Maybe a full minute. She paused on the camera bag and shook her head.

"If she's your aunt, I'm the Easter Bunny," she said at last.

"I don't know what you're talking about."

"I think you do."

The woman took a step forward. She was significantly shorter than Betty, but at the moment she seemed to tower over her. There was a seriousness in her eyes, something hard-edged and fierce. "You just tried to break into a government office," she said. "That's a felony. But I'm guessing you already knew that."

"I'm just here to see my aunt…"

"You knew it was a felony, but you did it anyway," the woman said, taking another step. "So one can only assume that a photograph of that body is worth more to you than a jail sentence. Does that sound about right?"

Betty held up her hands. "Look, I…"

"I doubt you'd stick your neck out like this for an animal attack," the woman said. "I mean, I'm sure there's a market for that sort of photo, but you don't strike me as a ghoul. Does that sound correct as well? Are you a ghoul?"

"No."

"Then who are you?"

"My name's Betty."

"Betty what?"

"Betty Roy."

The woman thought a moment then stuck out her hand. "I'm Dr Gail Cooper," she said as they shook. "Now tell me who you work for."

Betty started to answer then stopped herself. "You don't wanna know," she said.

"Spit it out."

"The Midnight Extra."

"Oh lord."

"I know, I know."

"The Elvis magazine?"

"Yeah," Betty said. "The Elvis magazine, but what's happening now is a lot bigger than that." She lowered her voice, just in case. "We went to see Mrs Vivet a couple days ago," she said. "The woman was nuts."

"You spoke with her?"

"Yeah. We spent the night in her garage. She called the Extra because she thought something was after her. And it definitely wasn't a bear."

Dr Cooper nodded to herself.

"I've stumbled across quite a mystery here," she said. "A real puzzle. You may have a few of the missing pieces."

"I'll tell you what I know."

A door opened from somewhere unseen within the building. They heard hard footsteps echo through the hallway, then another door opening and closing. Dr Cooper held her hand in the air until the silence returned.

"Not here," she said, pulling up the sleeve of her scrubs to check the time on her watch. "Definitely not here." She looked up to Betty and then down to the camera bag. "That camera stays out of your hands, understood?"

"Yeah."

"I mean it."

"So do I."

Dr Cooper nodded. "Alright," she said. "Just follow me and keep quiet. And I hope to God you have a strong stomach."

* * *

THEY WALKED through a series of white hallways with white walls and white drop ceilings. The building reminded Betty of a hospital, only colder. Purpose-built and unyielding. There weren't even any windows. Just tile and painted block and stainless steel.

Dr Cooper led them through a wide set of double doors and onto the floor of the main autopsy room. Betty followed a few steps behind, taking it all in. The rows of perforated steel tables. The full wall of sinks. Hanging scales like the scales at a grocery store, but so much larger and Betty stopped at one for just a moment and saw the cold metal basin and thought of all it had held. Her legs felt weak. Dr Cooper noticed and turned and waited. "It's just an autopsy room," she said.

"I've never been in one."

"Did you ever dissect a frog in science class?"

"No."

"Well I don't know what to tell you," Dr Cooper said. "Nothing here can hurt you, if that helps. And you're going to see more than empty scales and empty tables in a minute so you better toughen up." She went to a small door to the rear of the autopsy room and held it open. "Alright?"

Betty cleared her throat. "Yeah," she said.

"Good. Now come on, we don't have much time."

Everything was closer in the private autopsy room. The ceiling, the walls. The body on the table, hidden beneath a thick white sheet. The heavy smell of raw meat and disinfectant. Betty felt assaulted by all of it. She wanted to stay beside Dr Cooper, but found herself nearly pressed against the cabinets along the back wall instead. She could see the shape of Mrs Vivet's head and shoulders beneath the sheet.

If Dr Cooper noticed her discomfort she paid it no mind. She flipped a switch on the wall to turn on a pair of surgical lights above the autopsy table. Then she locked the door.

"I came in early this morning to work through a backlog," she said. "When I got to Mrs Vivet here I saw that the deputy coroner listed her as a wild animal attack. Should have been simple. No autopsy required. That's how it goes when there's no mystery. You can keep the knives in the drawer, so to speak. And who could fathom any mystery in a bear attack?"

Dr Cooper turned to Betty and saw the look on her face. "Hey," she said. "You with me?"

"Yeah," Betty managed.

"Well you certainly don't look like it. Is it the smell?"

"That's part of it."

Dr Cooper shook her head and went to one of the cabinets along the far wall and stood on a stool to reach a dusty jar of Vick's VapoRub on the second shelf. She climbed down and handed it to Betty.

"You can rub that under your nose if you want," she said. "The body's not really in decomp, but there's always a smell. Especially when the viscera has been torn open, like Mrs Vivet here. I'd say if you can stand it right now you'll be fine."

"It's ok."

"I don't even notice it anymore, but some people really lose it. I'd rather smell Vapor Rub than your breakfast."

"I'll be fine."

Dr Cooper looked at the wall clock. "Good," she said. "Now let's get moving. We have to make this quick."

"Why?"

"Well that's just one more part of the mystery. This body is tagged for 'specialized off-site examination.' Don't ask me what that means because I've never seen it. Fifteen years as a forensic pathologist and I've never heard of such a thing. Off-site examination and the pickup is at eight. I only noticed it after I started the autopsy and went digging for more information on Mrs Vivet here. It was particularly bad timing on my part since the tag also said not to touch the body." Dr Cooper looked at Betty and raised her eyebrows. "And I've never seen that either."

She held the sheet by the top edge, just beyond the lump of the head.

"You ready to see this?"

Betty walked closer to the table and nodded.

"You're sure."

"Yeah."

Dr Cooper folded the sheet neatly down, like she was turning down a bed, exposing what remained of Mrs Vivet. The open skull and wet brain beneath. The jagged lesions, the exposed muscle and fat. A great Y-shaped cut ran across the chest and the ribs were open and the organs bared and suddenly the world pulled in dark at the borders of Betty's vision and then darker still and she fell backward into the room.

Dr Cooper just watched as she fell. "I thought you said you were ready," she said.

Betty lay there on the floor.

Dr Cooper sighed and dropped the sheet and went to a cabinet along the rear wall. She found the box of smelling salts and removed a single packet and dropped down to her knees and cracked it open beneath Betty's nose. The effect was immediate. The heavy ammonia smell pierced through whatever fog had fallen over Betty and seemed to stab something inside her skull. She jerked away from Dr Cooper like she was holding a weapon.

"What the hell!"

"You said you were ready."

"Oh my God. That smell."

Dr Cooper held the packet up with two fingers and waved it in the air. Then she stood up and tossed it in the open trash bin. "I suppose I should be kinder about all of this," she said. "If not for your sake than mine."

Betty pushed herself up and brushed off her jeans. "This job takes a special kind of someone, doesn't it?"

"It does. Now are you finished being squeamish?"

Betty looked at the body again. She shivered, but did her best to hide it. "Yeah," she said.

"You're made of the same stuff, you know. It's just bones and muscle and fat and blood. Proteins and minerals."

Betty felt like she was more, but she kept that to herself. "Proteins and minerals," she said.

"Organic compounds, if you want to drill down further. Atoms and chemical bonds."

"Cold science," Betty said.

"If you like. Now look here."

Betty walked to the edge of the table to see where Dr Cooper was pointing.

"So the first thing I noticed, aside from the obvious trauma, was her skin. Look how perfect. I mean absolutely flawless. Like a baby's. This woman was in her forties but she has the skin of a newborn. Now I suppose you could mark that up to good genes and avoiding the sun, but it's incredibly unlikely. Not impossible though, so that's what I assumed. We're trained to always be sceptics of the impossible. We look for the logic."

She moved one of the surgical lights to shine into the chest cavity.

"But there is no logic that can explain what's inside the body. Remember, I was just looking for cause of death, so by this point I had not moved on to a full autopsy. But it's easy to get a glimpse of a person's liver when it's been partially pulled out of their abdomen. I saw immediately how perfect it was. Ignoring the bite marks, of course."

"Of course."

"Even a teetotaler with the healthiest diet would show some signs of age in their liver, but her's is perfect. It isn't an anomaly, it's simply impossible. So I went ahead and made the Y and took out the chest plate and guess what?"

Betty realized she was actually waiting for an answer. "The other organs were perfect too?"

Dr Cooper seemed pleased. "Absolutely flawless," she said. "Except for the bite marks."

She looked at the body for a long moment, shaking her head.

"So at this point I checked this woman's records. She isn't a Jane Doe. We have her full medical history on file. And guess where Mrs Vivet was just a few months ago?"

"Where?"

"The cancer ward at Piermont. In a persistent vegetative state."

"A coma?"

Dr Cooper nodded. "Caused by an intracranial tumor."

"She had brain cancer?"

"Aggressive. And that's where our records end."

"How?"

"Because her husband checked her out of the hospital for home hospice care. And that's the last anyone heard of Mrs Vivet until this body came in last night. She left the hospital with an inoperable tumor in her brain, and there's no hiding that. So I grabbed the cranial saw to have myself a peek. And guess what?"

She tapped Mrs Vivet's forehead with her finger.

"No tumor," Betty guessed.

"No sign of it whatsoever. Another impossibility. And then I found something else. This poor woman's brain is severely damaged, but not from age or disease or any other natural cause. Here, look. You can see scarring along the prefrontal cortex, here and here and here. Running along the anterior of the frontal lobes. Both are severed."

"Severed?"

"Cut."

"I know what severed means," Betty said. "I just don't know why they would be cut."

"Because she's been lobotomized."

"Oh my god."

"Multiple times from what I can tell. These scars here at the corners of both eyes tell you all you need to know." She pulled at the lids, but Betty didn't get close enough to see. Dr Cooper moved to Mrs Vivet's lower jaw and opened it to expose the teeth. "Her molars show stress fractures as well," she said. "Which I think could be the result of very high current electroshock. And this bite on her lower lip is very likely self-inflicted. Maybe during a procedure, or maybe before, I can't tell."

She stepped back and folded her arms.

"Alright, your turn. Tell me something that makes sense. Tell me why a woman in her forties has no signs of aging whatsoever. And tell me why someone would work so hard on rewiring her brain."

"You didn't mention the bear attack."

Dr Cooper actually laughed. "I suppose I didn't," she said. "What does that say when a fatal animal attack is the most ordinary part of an investigation." She nodded to the great cuts that ran the length of Mrs Vivet's body, and to the deep bites on the neck and shoulder. "It wasn't a bear. That's all I can tell you. I'm not a zoologist, but this thing was mean and strong and its bite is stretched further than any bear's on this earth. More like a snake with its jaw unhinged."

She folded her arms again.

"Your turn."

Betty hesitated. "This stays between us."

"Just like everything I told you."

"And you already said you believed me. So you have to keep that going. I've seen some impossible stuff too."

"Try me."

So Betty told her what she knew. All of it. Splitting cats included. She told her about the dazed and erratic woman they met and how they watched that same woman grow from the body of another. She told her about the creature stalking the house, and how it seemed to be splitting as well. And when she finished, Dr

Cooper still stood there with her arms crossed, nodding her head and looking at the body.

"You think I'm crazy," Betty said.

"Yesterday I would have."

"So what do we do now?"

Dr Cooper thought for a moment. "Any idea where the husband went?"

"No."

"And you think whatever killed this woman came out of that same lab."

"Where else?"

"I wouldn't doubt it. This kind of rapid tissue generation seems like it would be near impossible to control. This body is perfect, but I can imagine that any sort of contaminant could make a real mess."

"You can say that again."

"Well I also think there's only one person on God's green earth who knows what to do if that's the case."

"Dr Vivet."

Dr Cooper nodded. "I think you better find the husband," she said. "If he's your Doctor Frankenstein he may know how to stop the monster. Beyond that I'd say he has some pretty big things to contribute to medical science."

"You didn't see the video," Betty said, shaking her head. "You didn't see how she was. The way she looked at the things around her. Like she hated them. Like she was just evil. That must be why he cut into her brain. He was trying to fix her. Trying to turn her back into his wife."

"She was never his wife to begin with."

Betty didn't argue. She looked at the woman on the table and felt some sadness for her that she couldn't place. A fearful pity. As though she were a wild animal beaten into the circus.

Dr Cooper folded the sheet back up over the woman's face. She checked the clock again and turned the lights off. Together they walked back through the main autopsy floor and toward the rear entrance of the building. When Dr Cooper opened the emergency exit the outside air swept into the hall and smelled so sweet Betty wanted to drink it.

"I found info on Dr Vivet when I looked through Michelle's records. He's listed as a professor at Brabane University. You know where that is?"

"Vaguely."

"Well ask someone for directions," Dr Cooper said. "He works in the genetics department. If you want the next piece of this puzzle I think that's where you'll find it." She looked at Betty a moment, then looked out at the same empty view she had been contemplating earlier in the day. "I deal in puzzles," she said eventually. "Each body is a puzzle to solve and I am the one who solves them. You could call it a passion. What I've seen today has no solution and that is something I can't stand."

"I'll let you know what I find out."

"Please do."

Betty figured that was as close to a goodbye as Dr Cooper was going to get, so she started down the steps without another word. Dr Cooper watched her go. When she reached the bottom of the stairs Dr Cooper called her name and Betty turned and held a hand up to block the sun.

"You weren't here," she said. "Remember that. We never spoke."

"Got it."

"Alright," Dr Cooper said. "Now stay safe. And for for God's sake don't even think about printing my name in The Midnight Extra."

X

BUCK UP

The wail of police sirens stirred Buck from his restless dreams. No logic to them. Faces and screaming. A winter sky. And now the cold floor against his cheek. Hard and cold. He just stared at it. Dirty checkered linoleum. Chair legs of a design he didn't recognize, cheap and dirty as the floor. Smell of stale smoke. The dreams were gone and forgotten. The sirens persisted. His head was throbbing in time.

"Ah shit," he said.

Years of old bubblegum clustered like fungus on the table above him. Cobwebs at the corners of the legs. He slid out from beneath it and propped himself against the nearest wall. The sirens finally stopped. Early sunshine fell through a wide front window. Hanging silhouettes of beer logos. An open sign gone dark. He looked at his watch and sighed.

His mouth tasted as foul as it ever had. Like bitter ashes. He managed to stand and survey the empty bar. Flashes of light and he thought he might pass out so he gripped the table with both hands and hung his head. A note on the table from Linda: *Get well soon Bucko.*

Damn but his head was throbbing. He walked behind the bar and grabbed a pint glass and filled it with water at the sink and drank it. His mouth was so dry the water burned. He filled it again and drank again. The drawer beneath the cash register was where Linda kept her smokes and he hoped like hell she kept some aspirin there as well.

She did. He took the bottle and shook out two pills and swallowed them with a drink of the water and then he swallowed two more for good measure. He stuck the bottle in his jacket pocket.

"I owe you," he said to the empty bar.

He saw the liquor all lined up there against the mirror and felt hunger and revulsion in equal measure and he turned his back to them and took his water and sat at the nearest booth.

Faint memories of the night before came in little fits and spurts. Shatner on the television. Some fancy drink. They trickled away beyond a certain point and he found no memory of the bar closing. Another drink of the water and he noticed for the first time the vomit on his sweatpants. Betty's sweatpants. And the thought of it was so shameful that he sat there and cried. Damn but there was no aspirin for shame.

The bathroom of the Crow's Nest smelled like Janet Lane's office and he wasn't sure if it was the smell or the association but something made his stomach turn. He ran to the nearest stall and threw up all the water he had been drinking. The aspirin too. He wiped his mouth with his hand and went to the sink and in the dirty mirror he saw himself with his black eye and unshaven face and near sixty years of worry written along the wrinkles. A mask he couldn't take off. And what was it Rathbone said about the inner not matching the outer?

Rathbone.

He stood staring at the mirror but he wasn't seeing himself at all.

Rathbone.

Christ he had forgotten the whole conversation. Good God.

He washed his hands and cupped them beneath the faucet and splashed water on his face again and again. More and more of the night coming into focus. Something about the doctor and that thing and how they were one and the same. How it was coming for him. Jesus, he'd forgotten about all of it. He turned off the faucet and went out to each booth along the wall and checked the ashtrays for Rathbone's torn up business card. He found nothing. A phone hung on the wall behind the bar and he ran to it to call Betty only to realize he didn't have her number. He called *The Midnight Extra* instead.

"Newsroom."

"Hey Sammy it's Buck."

"Hey Buck. Damn if you don't sound like you've had a rough one."

"Rough was only the beginning."

"Well you've got another half hour to sober up. She's on the warpath. No content coming from your section and the clock is ticking."

"I'm out for the day Sammy. I've got a scoop. A real one. If you see her you can tell her that."

"And put my neck on the block? I don't think so bub."

"Well she can blow all the steam she wants. When this story cracks it'll sell so hot she'll need a double run."

"Well damn Buck I hope so."

"Hey listen Sammy, can you poke your head over and see if Betty's made it to the office yet?"

"I can see from here. Photography's empty, but it's still early."

Buck checked his watch. "Not that early," he said.

"Well maybe she's out chasing her own hot lead you know?"

"Yeah maybe. Hey do me a favor and grab her number from the directory for me will ya?"

"Yeah one sec."

Buck jotted the number down on a bar napkin. He noticed his hands were shaking.

"Got it?"

"Yeah I got it. Keep an eye out for her alright? If she comes in just tell her to hang tight. Tell her not to leave the office. You got that?"

"Well I don't know Betty like you do Buck, but I doubt she'd respond very well to that."

"Yeah well it's important. Can you tell her that? Tell her it's important."

"Just to stay put?"

"Yeah."

"Well sure, I'll tell her."

"Thanks Sammy. Hey one more thing."

"Shoot."

"I need some info on a couple guys. You feel like doing some sleuthing?"

"Yeah sure, give me the names."

"Dr Steven Vivet."

"Vivet? That crazy woman's husband?"

"One and the same."

"Got eaten by your hellhound I thought."

Buck forced a laugh.

"I need to know where he worked. Which hospital. Department, that sort of thing."

"Yeah I'll see what I can dig up."

"The other name is Rathbone."

"Rathbone?"

"Yup. Godfrey Rathbone."

"Hell of a name. Any idea where to start?"

"He seemed like a real blowhard. Scholarly type, you know?"

"Boy, you're not giving me much to go on."

"Whatever you can find."

"Alright I'm on top of it."

"I appreciate it."

"You got it Bucko. Stay safe out there."

He kept the handset pressed to his ear and pressed the switch on the base of the phone and listened for the dial tone. He dialed Betty's number from the napkin and let it ring and ring. No answer.

He hung up the phone and made for the door. He wondered how he would lock it after he left, then realized he needed a key to open it in the first place.

"Well damn," he said, tapping the lock with his knuckle.

Two squad cars were pulled up to the curb just outside the bar. Buck saw them through the window in the door. Their lights were off and three police officers stood in a small huddle with a woman smoking a cigarette. Buck recognized her immediately as

Linda. She turned and pointed toward the bar with her cigarette and Buck caught her eye and pounded on the window and called out her name.

The officers all turned. He could see Linda mouth a string of curse words before excusing herself to unlock the door.

"Well damn Buck, I figured you'd sleep until noon."

"Hey Linda."

"Hey yourself."

He knew how he looked and he could only imagine how he'd acted the night before. He looked her in the eyes and said a heartfelt thanks and she must have believed it. Her face softened and she told him not to mention it.

"I would have called you a cab, to be honest," she said. "But your friend was really persistent."

"Rathbone?"

Linda shrugged. "That guy in the suit. I had him pegged for an asshole, but he paid your room and board."

"He did?"

"Yeah, gave me five hundred bucks to let you sleep it off. He gave Jake the same. Told me not to tell you. Strange guy. You know he stood out at the front door for some time before he came in last night? Just stood there looking at the door. Checking it like he wanted to know how tough it was. Really creeped out the girls at the window bar, but damn if he wasn't onto something."

"What do you mean?"

Linda cocked her head. "Aren't you wondering why the police are here? Turn around."

Buck stepped from the doorway and turned to look at the building. His stomach turned again when he saw the deep gouges clawed across the facade. They swept across the door and masonry in great arcs. Four lines apiece, spaced out just like the cuts on his leg.

"Good lord," Buck whispered.

"Something wanted to get in the bar last night," Linda said. "Wanted to get in there real bad. Police said there's been bear attacks, but I'll be damned if that looks like something a bear would do."

One of the officers broke away from the group and walked up to Buck and Linda. He nodded to Buck and asked him if he'd been in the bar all night. The question seemed like a formality. One look at Buck and you'd know the answer.

Buck started to reply but Linda waved the officer away.

"Won't do you no good talking to him," she said. "Thing coulda broken in and swallowed him whole. He was out."

The officer seemed to agree. He told Linda they had more questions and she said goodbye to Buck and told him to straighten out.

He headed toward his car, turning back twice along the way to look at the deep gouges in the door. He scanned the tops of the buildings as well.

*   *   *

His apartment was small and modest. A bedroom, a living room, a kitchen. An old sofa and an older TV. When he first moved in he believed it would only be temporary. It was a notion he held for the next twenty years. The walls were bare save for a single bootprint cast in plaster that hung behind the sofa. No houseplants, no pets. Always the same four dishes in and out of the sink. The same rotation of food in the refrigerator.

A bottle of whisky sat on the counter and Buck went to it immediately. He had smelled his own vomit on Betty's sweatpants the entire drive home and he became so filled with the shame of it he could only see that bottle in his mind's eye. As if he were driving toward it and it alone. He unscrewed the cap and poured it down the kitchen drain and threw away the empty bottle like it was itself a dangerous thing. The kitchen filled with the smell of the whiskey and for the first time in ages the smell didn't make him want more. It made him sick to his stomach and he ran to the bathroom and threw up all over again.

He took a shower so hot and so long that he could barely see for all the steam. Like a sweat lodge. A deep cleanse down to the pores. Damn if he didn't need it.

He saw the dark spectre of his black eye in the fogged mirror and he felt like he deserved it and decided he would wear it proudly. He shaved, brushed his teeth, then brushed them a second time. Then he got dressed and called The Midnight Extra.

"Newsroom."

"Hey Sammy, you get eyes on Betty yet?"

"Hey Bucko. Nope, I've seen neither hide nor hair. Checked with photography and she hasn't reported to them either."

"Got it. You remember what I said?"

"Yeah, yeah. Keep her here if she shows up. Hey listen, I turned a few things up with your names."

"Yeah, what'd you find?"

"Well I started with the doctor. Checked every hospital within fifty miles. No record at all. Never heard of the guy. I can keep on it if you want, but it seemed like a dead end.

"Damn."

"Yeah well thats the bad news. Good news is I checked on this Rathbone fella. Figured that university on the hill was a good place to start and I'll be damned if it wasn't a hit. Lady on the phone knew the name without even looking it up. Godfrey Rathbone. Said he was the... hang on I wrote it down... She said he was the Chancellor Emeritus, whatever the hell that is. Smart college stuff is all I can figure."

"Good work Sammy."

"So there you go. You owe me."

He tried calling Betty's apartment one last time, then he got in his car and sped away.

XI

THE UNIVERSITY

BRABANE UNIVERSITY housed eleven separate buildings, all gathered upon the top of a wide and heavily wooded hill along the southern edge of the Eldent River Valley. The University was founded in 1961 but the buildings were far older. Buck could see their grey stone walls and turrets breaking above the treeline like exposed teeth as he drove the Volvo up the narrow forest road.

He passed a wide iron gate at the crest of the hill and followed the road down a long central promenade that ended at the same great cathedral he had always seen from The Midnight Extra's parking lot. Twenty-nine years he had been staring at that thing, and here it was looming at the end of the road. It was a lot bigger up close. Scarier too. Like it didn't belong among the smaller buildings. Like it would just swallow up the packs of well-dressed students traveling the walkways and gardens and plazas beneath it.

His thoughts drifted into even darker places and he found himself halfway down the promenade before he realized he had no idea where he was going. He checked the rearview then slowed the Volvo and pulled over to the side of the road. He sat there with his hands on the wheel, looking at each building in turn, wondering why the hell none of them had signs. He knew Rathbone was expecting him and he knew he could probably ask one person and be done with it. What he didn't know was if he really wanted to see Rathbone at all. That awful smile.

"I know you're probably up there, Lugosi," he said to the cathedral. "But I think I'll do some digging first."

He was watching a flock of dark birds weave along the upper spires of the building when he heard a tapping sound on his window. He turned to see a campus police officer staring at him. The man was young and heavyset. Stone-faced behind his mirrored sunglasses.

"That was fast," Buck muttered as he cranked the window down.

"Afternoon sir."

"Officer."

"Can I ask what your business is on campus today?"

Buck smiled. "Just running a little late to class."

The officer's expression didn't change.

"Sir I'll ask you again. What is your business on campus today?"

"I'm just visiting," Buck said. "My daughter is considering this lovely school and I wanted to get a lay of the land."

"Your daughter sir?"

Buck thought a moment. He did the math. Sometimes you just forget.

"Granddaughter," he said.

"And have you scheduled your visit?"

"Nope. I came here to do just that."

"You can schedule a visit by telephone."

"Well I'm sure I could, but I didn't. Can you point me in the right direction?"

"You see that turn up ahead?"

The officer pointed to a break in the wooded parkway that ran between the lanes.

"Yeah, I see it."

"Well that's where you can turn your car around and go back the way you came."

Buck watched the officer a moment, then looked at the road ahead. He started to argue when the radio strapped near the officer's shoulder squelched and through the static fuzz he heard the dispatcher say a series of numbers that seemed to get the officer's attention. He gripped the radio and leaned toward it, turning away from the car and cocking his head. Buck sat back in the seat and tapped on the steering wheel.

The officer's face appeared through the window a few moments later. "Visitor lot is just up ahead," he said with a smile.

Buck just stared at him.

"You'll want to take the second right and sign in at the gatehouse. They'll give you a visitor pass. Then you just follow the walk to the cathedral. You can't miss it. Sound good?"

"I mean…"

"You have a nice day now. Enjoy your visit."

And with that he turned and walked on down the sidewalk. Buck watched him go then leaned forward and looked cautiously at the trees and lamposts and statues that lined the road.

His name was already on the guest list when he arrived at the gatehouse. The attendant handed him a pass for his dashboard and a badge for his shirt and told him he was expected at the cathedral.

Only the cathedral. She really stressed that part. Then she smiled and waved him through. He didn't know what to say so he didn't say anything. He got out of his car and stood there in the open lot.

"What in the hell?" he said to himself.

He was about to head out when he caught sight of his own reflection in the passenger side window. The black eye stood out like face paint. Nothing subtle about it. The old fedora lay on the dashboard where Betty had left it and he considered it a moment then opened the door and put it on. It felt like he had never taken it off in the first place. The comforting weight of it. How the checkered satin lining felt cool against his head. He checked his reflection once more then cocked the brim down to one side to hide the black eye and stood there like the harrowed ghost of his younger self. It was the best he'd felt in a long, long time.

"Hot damn," he said.

Halfway to the cathedral he watched a group of students veer from the main walkway. They all wore long white labcoats and Buck immediately thought of the grainy image of Dr Vivet from the videos. He checked all around for any sign of someone watching, then he sauntered after them at a distance, walking casually with his hands in his trouser pockets as they headed toward a grey stone tower that reached just above the treeline. The building reminded Buck of something from ancient Rome. The columned sides and high stacked tiers of arched windows. A grandeur so out of place in the town Buck had always known. The students, for their part, seemed unmoved. They hung around the bases of the columns for a short time before disappearing into the entryway of the building. Buck watched them go. Then he took the visitor badge from his shirt and put it in his pocket and followed them inside.

The mosaic floor and vaulted entryway reminded Buck of the church his mother would attend when he was very young. The darkness of it. How the air was always cold. Smell of dust and candle smoke. He stood a moment at the threshold, watching as the students filed down a long corridor that split the entirety of the first floor. They broke off and vanished into rooms along the hall and Buck followed after them. He walked slowly, peering into the rooms as he passed. Each a lecture hall as grand as the building itself. High stone ceilings and ringed tiers of hardwood benches that made Buck think of old oil paintings he had only ever seen in books. The alien way the professors dressed, with their black robes and high white collars. He thought that he had never seen someone dressed so odd. Then again, he had never set foot in a fancy school.

"Smart people stuff," he muttered to himself.

The students filed down the rows of seats and quietly took their places and sat with notepads and pencils at the ready. The professor situated himself behind a wooden lectern and began flipping the pages in a large book. Blackboards were stacked behind the man and covered with symbols Buck had never seen. He studied them a moment, wondering how the professor could even reach the upper heights of the boards when his thoughts were interrupted by the static click and hiss of a police radio. When he turned he saw an officer standing in the far entryway.

A pair of display cases stood on ether side of the lecture hall door and Buck crept behind the nearest one and pressed himself against the wall. He waited a moment then leaned forward to peer around the edge. The officer had not moved. His radio crackled and some message was relayed that Buck could not make out and the officer grabbed the radio to reply then started down the corridor.

Buck pressed back against the wall as the footsteps grew louder and louder. Another squelch of the radio. He looked toward the rear entrance, but there was no way to make it. He looked into the packed lecture hall where the professor had just begun attendance.

"Ah shit," he said. "Shit, shit, shit."

He took a deep breath and walked confidently into the hall. Head held high. The professor glanced up from his attendance sheet, watching Buck from above his horn rimmed glasses.

"Excuse me," the professor said.

Buck just kept walking.

"Sir? Excuse me. You can't be here."

Buck had no idea what to do so he just gave the man a smile and a big thumbs up and kept walking. He scanned the room for another doorway but saw nothing. He started to sweat. "It's ok," he said. "Don't stop on my account."

The professor glared at him. "Sir there is no reason you should be in my classroom," he said. "Absolutely no reason."

Buck kept walking. He could feel the eyes of the students watching him.

The professor threw his hands up and looked to the back row of seats. He snapped his fingers. "Jason," he called. "Can you please get security?"

A student stood immediately.

"Now that won't be necessary," Buck said. "I'm just here for inspection."

"Inspection of what?"

"Well… I'm just checking your emergency exits. You have one, of course?"

The professor looked at Buck a long moment then gestured with his hand toward the far edge of the stage. "Behind the stage, but this is extremely inappropriate."

Buck started to run. He reached the end of the central aisle and turned right then headed for the stage and the unmarked doorway carved into the stone wall behind it. "You really should have it marked!" he yelled behind him.

The doorway led to a wide curving hallway covered in oil paintings and overflowing with sunlight. Buck stopped and his shoes squealed on the polished floor and he turned left then right with no idea which way to go. He heard a voice shouting behind him and knew there was no time at all so he trusted his gut and ran to the left, hoping it would lead to the entrance. It led to a great wooden staircase instead.

"Ah shit," he said, frantically out of breath. He put his hands on his knees and tried to take a deep breath but he heard footsteps running on the stone floor behind him so he shot up the stairs two at a time. They led up and up and finally ended at a second curved hallway, nearly identical to the one below. He turned and headed down the hallway, past a series of closed doors with names painted across their frosted glass windows.

The footsteps were coming up the stairs. Heavy and loud and growing closer. Buck tried the door handles as he ran. One after the other. Again and again he found them locked until finally one turned and he shoved the door open and pulled it shut and flipped the brass deadbolt and dropped to the ground with his back pressed against the door.

He waited. His heart was pounding and his breaths came in heavy gasps and when he heard the footsteps echo down the hall he tried to hold them in as long as he could.

The sounds came and went without stopping. He could hear the voice on the radio and the officer's voice in reply, both getting further and further away. And then he heard nothing at all.

He took a few deep breaths, then grunted as he pushed himself to his feet. He brushed himself off and straightened his tie and was just about to flip the deadbolt and open the door when he read the name painted in bold letters across the glass. They were written backward, but easy enough to read:

Dr. Steven Vivet

"Well I'll be damned," he said to the empty room. "I will be goddamned."

A shuffling came from somewhere in the depths of the dark office. A creaking sound. Buck turned to the noise but the faint light from the window barely penetrated the shadows and he squinted to see a tall wardrobe standing alone in the farthest corner. The sound came again and as he watched he saw the wardrobe door slowly open.

Buck pressed himself to the door. His hand reached blindly for the handle, but he couldn't find it and when he finally did he grabbed it and turned and forgot about the deadbolt. He jerked at the door and frantically searched for the lock and had just enough time to find it when he heard a familiar voice.

"Buck?"

He froze.

"Buck what the hell are you doing here?"

He could barely make out her shape for all the dark, but her voice was unmistakable.

"Betty?"

XII

THE OFFICE OF DR VIVET

SHE EMERGED from the shadows of the office and leaned against the cluttered desk that occupied the center of the room. Her camera was slung loose over her shoulder and she slid it off and placed it on a stack of papers beside her.

"You didn't piss yourself again, did you?"

There wasn't enough light to tell if she was smiling.

"Goddamn it Betty."

"Oh what, did I scare you? Well you scared the hell out of me. How did you even find this place?"

Buck collapsed into a swivel chair facing the desk and waited for his heart to stop pounding. He couldn't remember the last time he ran up a flight of stairs. He leaned his head back and Betty saw his face in the dim light and noticed his eye for the first time.

"Ah damn it Buck, I'm sorry."

"For what?"

"For punching you in the face. Your eye looks awful."

He made a dismissive motion with his hand, as though pushing the words away.

"I deserved it."

"Not really."

"Well if not from you then from someone else."

"I'm still sorry."

Buck was silent a long time. He stood and shrugged his jacket from his shoulders then sat back down and rolled up his shirt-sleeves. When he finally spoke his voice was somber.

"Yeah well I'm sorry too. I've had some time to think about things, and what I said last night… if I could take it back I would."

He leaned forward and propped his elbows on his knees. The light only touched half his face and the shadows it cast beneath his eyes made him look ancient. He held his hands together and pressed them to his chin.

"It's ok," Betty said.

"No it isn't. You're not a kid."

"Really it's ok."

"Just listen."

He searched for the right words but knew they wouldn't come. He took off the fedora and sat it on his knee and ran a hand through his hair. His heart had stopped that awful thudding and his breath was returning to normal. He looked at Betty and the Pentax camera beside her. Always there beside her.

"It's hard to see how far you've fallen," he said. "It happens so slowly that you don't even notice. And if you do see a hint of it you can just play it off. Hide it away. You do that long enough and the years just vanish. I don't know why I'm seeing it now but I am. Time just moves in the one direction. It doesn't care how you spend it. Does that make any sense?"

"Not really."

Buck couldn't help but smile.

"I kind of gave up after Willie died," he said. "And I never really came back. I don't think I wanted to. I guess I didn't see the point."

"So what changed?"

"I met you. And you actually give a damn about something. And I haven't cared about anything in so long I forgot what it felt like. It's made me take a look at myself and it's not pretty. But it's all I got. And I'm done scraping around the bottom. I wasted the last twenty years of my life. I don't want to waste the next twenty."

"Well that's being generous," Betty said.

Buck laughed again. Damn but it felt good to laugh. "And I'm glad we're partners," he said. "I really am. You're a tough cookie, you know that? You got real grit. That hasn't stopped me from being worried sick about you though."

Betty smiled in the dark.

"You get kind of sappy when you're hungover, huh?"

Buck just shook his head.

"You said that about me being drunk too."

"Maybe you're just a sap."

"Maybe I am. But I care about you. I can't see you get hurt."

They sat there in the dark. A clock ticked away from some wall in the office. Neither had noticed it before.

"You would have liked my grandad," Betty said eventually.

"Yeah?"

"He was a sap too."

Buck watched her a moment. The way she only looked at the floor or somewhere in the far distance. He could see how glassy her eyes had gone.

"You really miss him," he said.

Betty just nodded. It was about all she could do. She wiped her eyes with the back of her hand and clenched her jaw.

"Yeah, I really do."

Buck nodded. There really wasn't much more to say about it.

"I shaved," he said.

Betty cocked her head.

"I showered and shaved and took some aspirin and put on clean clothes."

"So?"

"So how the hell can you tell I'm hungover? I thought I was hiding it pretty well."

Betty smiled and wiped her hand over her eyes again and took a breath.

"Oh please," she said. "So what did you do? Leave my place and go straight to the bar?"

"Sure did. Woke up on the floor."

She gave him a look. He could barely see it in the shadows. Worry and sadness with no small amount of pity. He shook his head.

"I know."

"On a Wednesday, Buck?"

"It was a rough day."

"Yeah I remember."

"Well it ended up being fortuitous."

"Fortuitous?"

"Yeah, lucky."

"I know what it means. How was getting slammed on a Wednesday night lucky?"

"Because that white haired guy decided to stop by for a chat. Rathbone."

"Seriously?"

Buck nodded.

"He works here too. He invited me up for a chat and I decided to do some digging first. He was a real wacko."

"What'd he say?"

"A bunch of nonsense. Mostly."

"Mostly?"

"Well two things caught my attention. First off, that thing we've been chasing isn't Dr Vivet's experiment gone awry."

"No?"

"No. It's Dr Vivet."

Betty just looked at him. It took a second to sink in. She looked around the dark office and shivered.

"God damn," she said.

"Yeah."

"How?"

"I don't know. Whatever gibberish Rathbone told me didn't make any sense."

"Because you were drunk."

"No, because it was crazy. Something about experimenting on himself with his wife's dead blood. Just crazy talk."

"Dead blood?"

"Crazy talk. "

"What else did he say?"

Buck hesitated. He watched Betty a long moment.

"That bad, huh?"

"Well I told you this guy was nutty. So whatever he says shouldn't be taken too seriously, you know?"

"What did he say, Buck?"

"Just that Dr Vivet was going to hunt me down and kill me. Something along those lines."

"God damn."

"Yeah," Buck said.

"So after hearing that you thought it would be a good idea to get wasted."

"I was already pretty far gone."

"Jesus Christ."

"Yeah."

"Anything else?"

Buck thought a moment. "No," he said. "After that he took the tapes and left."

"He stole the tapes?"

"I let him take them."

"Did he threaten you?"

"Not really," Buck said. "Actually he was very polite. I think I was the asshole."

"Well that should get you on his good side."

"It didn't hurt. I found out this morning that he paid the bar staff to let me stay and sleep it off."

"Really?"

Buck nodded. He left out the part where the creature clawed through stone to try and reach him.

"Well while you were sleeping I went to the Medical Examiner's."

"They let you in?"

"Kind of."

And Betty told him about Dr Cooper and the autopsy and the damage to Mrs Vivet's brain. She left out the part where she nearly passed out. Buck listened with something like sadness on his face. "Love conquers," he said when she finished.

"What?"

"Something Rathbone said last night. How some things are so important you'd do anything to get them back."

Betty shrugged. "So now what?"

Buck thought a moment. "Well you know what Churchill said about going through hell, don't you?"

"Of course I don't."

Buck took the fedora from his knee and placed it on his head. "He said you gotta keep going."

Betty looked at Buck as he sat forward in the chair. Tweed jacket in the crook of his arm. The matching vest and paisley tie. Pressed white shirt with the sleeves rolled to the forearm and the fedora now cocked on his head. Looking for all the world like a reporter from some forgotten age. His black eye and hangover only added to the effect.

"Well then I better show you what I found," she said. "You're gonna love it."

She hopped off the desk and went to the wardrobe behind the desk. "You're blocking the light," she called.

Buck stood from the chair and stepped away from the window. He walked to the edge of the desk and stirred through the papers while Betty fumbled in the wardrobe. When she came over to him she was holding a snub-nosed revolver, pointing it at his chest.

"You know how to use one of these?"

Buck guided the barrel away.

"As a matter of fact, I do."

He held out a hand and Betty gave him the gun and he felt the weight of it. The polished hardwood grip fit perfectly into his hand. He flipped back the hammer and spun the cylinder. Five bullets in six chambers. He could smell the oil in the air.

"Did you know it was loaded?"

"Damn."

He settled the hammer above the empty chamber.

"Find any more bullets?"

Betty shook her head.

Buck tucked the revolver into his belt. "Why the hell would he have a gun?" he asked.

"No idea."

"You find anything else?"

"Not much. There's lots of books and stuff, but its too dark to read anything. I didn't want to turn on the light."

"Where's your trusty flashlight?"

"I dropped it when I saved you from being eaten."

Buck couldn't argue with that. He looked to the window and the faint light seeping in through it. Then he looked to the desk and the iron tape dispenser at its edge. He took the roll and began taping his jacket over the window. Betty came over and held it in place.

When they were done the office was left perfectly black and Buck fumbled his way to the desk and found the beaded chain dangling from the lamp. He pulled it and the office filled with warm amber light. It was far more cluttered in the light than Buck imagined in the dark. Glass-doored cabinets lined one wall, their shelves packed with specimen jars whose contents Buck could only guess at. He saw the fetal shapes and pale wormlike curves within the largest among them and didn't hazard a closer look. Along the rear wall sat two great bookshelves and he stood and went to them and browsed along the leather spines. The titles were almost indecipherable.

Something caught his eye on a lower shelf and he bent down for a closer look and saw a deep hole punched into the spine of one of the books. He took the book from the shelf and brought it to the desk and set it down beneath the lamp. When he opened it he found a bullet buried halfway through the pages.

He looked at the shelf where the book had been placed, then he looked to the desk and the chair seated behind it. The line he drew was clear.

He went to the back of the chair and parted the seams between the pleated leather and frowned.

"Ah Christ," he said.

Betty was rummaging around the desk. She turned at Buck's voice. "What?"

"I think he shot himself."

"Really?"

"Yeah."

He felt the cold metal of the revolver tucked in his belt and suddenly felt like throwing it on the floor.

"So you think he missed or something?"

"No," Buck muttered, remembering the hole in the back of the creature's head. "I just don't think it worked."

He rifled through the papers on the desk.

"What are you looking for?" Betty asked.

"Anything from the doctor. Like a note or something. You wouldn't take your life and not let the world know why."

He tipped out the contents of the trash can onto the floor and toed through them. Wrappers and papers and wadded up tissues. Nothing.

"Where was the gun?"

"I stepped on it."

"You what?"

"Yeah, he must have dropped it when he, you know." She made a finger gun and pointed it to her mouth.

Buck eased himself down to his knees and felt around the carpet by the chair and beneath the desk. His hand touched upon what felt like a small book and he grabbed it and brought it up to the desk.

"A journal?" Betty asked.

"Yeah I think so."

"Hot damn."

Buck smiled. He started flipping through the pages. Laboratory notes, personal observations, diagrams. Page after page of impenetrable text. Nothing. He noticed how each entry was dated along the top edge of the page. He turned to Betty.

"Do you remember the date stamp from the videos?"

Betty thought a moment. "Early December, I think."

Buck flipped through the months until he found the entries for December. He scanned the words, reading a few sentences out loud as he went:

Treatment going better than expected. No sign of host rejection of developing subdermal nodes.

-

First external node appeared along the anterior temporal line, showing perfect structure. The growth rhythm seems well within the projected tolerances. Slower than the felines, of course, but that was to be expected. Biopsy revealed ideal cellular generation. I am hopeful."

-

The first eye has finally opened and I cannot bear to look at it. The cellular composition is identical, but there is such a wild anomaly in temperment. It follows me around the room. It watches me with a malice that Michelle never possessed.

"Oh my god," Betty said.
Buck continued:

Restraints have been added out of necessity. It will not stop clawing at Michelle. I've stockpiled pentobarbital as a precaution if the restraints prove insufficient. Its strength is frightening. Inducing a coma may be my only option. The irony of this is not lost on me. I only hope that the wildness it displays is temporary. Part of early-stage cerebral development. I will know more as it matures.

Buck flipped further ahead.

Full separation occurred last week, but I am unwilling to decrease the pentobarbital. I do not want to wake it up again. The last time was too much to bear. I have buried Michelle and this beast has taken her place.

-

Rathbone knows the mysteries of the brain better than anyone I've ever known. He's agreed to help. He is fascinated by her. He has hope.

-

Surgery after surgery. Drug after drug. The malice is gone, but she is an awful, empty thing.

-

I have begged Rathbone for a second specimen, and he has delivered. Her blood is the key to regeneration, but she needs a healthy host. I know it. The tumor must have hindered the development. What else could it have been? She needs a healthy mind to grow from. Someone who loves her. Who holds her memory. It does not end like this. I won't let it.

Buck noticed how the handwriting began to rapidly deteriorate. It seemed to become more and more frantic as the entries went on.

Parasite. Something wrong. I feel it growing inside me. A new brain sprouting beside my own. It should not feel so cold. The thoughts it shares. Horrible, horrible. The seizures are painful and I cannot stop them. Teeth and hair falling out. I feel my temple itch.

It does not know about the gun. I am sorry.

Handwriting now little more than scratches. Spatter of blood on the page.

gone. lost. only hungry. where have i

Betty looked at the pages with her jaw slack. "That's the end?"

"Yeah."

"Can we get the hell out of here now?"

Buck nodded.

He went to the desk and pulled the chain on the lamp and the room fell to darkness once again. He went over to the door and unlocked the deadbolt, then grabbed the edge of his jacket.

"Ready?"

"Yeah."

He pulled down on the jacket and a shadow filled the glass. Someone was standing on the other side of the door. Just standing there. And the handle of the door began to turn.

Buck fell backward into the room. He had enough sense to kick out his foot to brace the door as he did so, holding it shut just as a crack of light appeared.

"Mr Vincent," a smooth, dry voice called from beyond the door. "Could you please open this door?"

Buck eased slightly.

"Rathbone?" Betty whispered.

Buck nodded.

"Mr. Vincent please. We're running out of time."

XIII

DREAMS

RATHBONE SMILED as he stepped inside the office. He looked at Buck standing there in the near dark with Betty at his side and he shook his head and clicked his tongue.

"Mr Vincent," he said. "This sneaking around does not suit you. If you wanted to visit Dr Vivet's office you needed only to ask." He turned to Betty and bowed his head. His eyes stayed locked with hers, shining like glass in the lamp light. His shadow stretched up the wall.

"Miss Roy," he said. "Charmed."

He didn't seem to expect a reply and none was given. He flipped the wall switch for the overhead lights and checked the time on his gold watch. He seemed far less menacing once the lights flickered on, almost fragile. Just a slender, tall, old man in a nice dark suit. An old friend of the family.

"I was expecting you earlier, Mr Vincent," he said. "But we still have some time. Come, I'll show you the grounds."

Buck didn't budge.

Rathbone looked at both of them and then down to the desk and the journal that lay open there among the clutter. He looked at it a moment, then nodded to himself.

"I can only imagine the tragedy you found in those pages," he said. "I can only imagine."

"What the hell is the specimen?" Betty said.

Rathbone thought for a long time. He seemed to struggle with the right words. "Why don't I show you," he said at last.

"It turned him into a monster."

"I would argue that he turned himself into a monster, Miss Roy. It certainly was not my intention. Now please, follow me."

Buck and Betty stayed right where they were.

"I think we'll pass," Buck said.

Rathbone's smile returned. "I don't bite," he said. "But Doctor Vivet's new wife does. It bites uncontrollably. And as soon as the sun has fallen it will come looking for you. I can promise you that. I'm sure it has thought of little else all day. Such is its mind."

"I can take care of myself."

"In certain matters perhaps, but not this one. Believe me."

"I made it this far."

"Not without my help," Rathbone said. "Luckily you will drink just about anything placed beneath your nose. Even chloral hydrate."

"You slipped me a Mickey?"

"I did. But only to keep you safe. If you had found your way home I believe the doctor's new wife would have come tearing through your front door."

"You want me to say thanks?"

"No, I want you to tell me how you plan on avoiding it tonight. Or tomorrow. Or all the days after that." He looked at the gun poking out from Buck's belt and nodded to it. "I doubt even that revolver will do much good," he said. "I believe it has already proven itself to be ineffective. You need other means, and I can supply them. Now come. Walk with me."

Another gesture with his hand. A gentle wave. As if Buck and Betty were his grandchildren and they were all heading to the park. He folded his hands behind his back and left the room and began to walk down the hall.

Buck and Betty shared a look. Buck shrugged. Betty held her hands up and in a moment they both left the room and followed behind Rathbone. He turned his head to watch them, slowing a moment so they could walk at his sides.

Walking the halls gave Buck a chance to see just how ornate the building was. Little details you couldn't catch when running from the police. Mosaic alcoves along the inner walls. Carved hardwood molding along the upper edges of the ceiling. It was like walking through a museum.

"This building houses our lecture halls and most of the faculty offices," Rathbone said. "I enjoy bringing the many disciplines and professors together under one roof. They tend to pollinate one another if you let them. Science in isolation has no imagination, and imagination is fruitless without the boundaries of science."

"And where do horrible mutants fit in?" Buck said.

Rathbone laughed his dry laugh. "Somewhere along the periphery of both," he said. "Out in the frontier."

They walked down the great turning staircase to the gallery on the lower floor. Rathbone guided them as though they had come exclusively for a tour of the building. He pointed out the classrooms in session and the artwork hanging salon-style on the wainscotted walls. Buck watched the paintings come and go with little interest. Rathbone seemed enamored with them, but there was little for Buck to get excited about. Most seemed to be romantic landscapes and classical portraits of the long dead. Yawn. One in particular dominated the wall near the gallery's end and Betty stopped in front of it with no encouragement from Rathbone. She couldn't help it.

"You have good taste, Miss Roy."

"What the hell is it?"

Buck had the same question. At first glance the painting showed a dark ocean and a blood red sky, but when he got closer he noticed the sea was roiling with life. Eyes and teeth like pinpricks of light among the dark water.

"One of mine," Rathbone said. He kept his hands folded behind his back and shifted his weight to his heels. "A personal favorite. I believe I recounted the vision quite well."

"I told you he was nutty," Buck said to Betty.

Rathbone laughed again. "Mr Vincent I do appreciate your candor," he said. "I truly do. It's refreshing. Sometimes we get so caught up in our endeavors we don't see them through anyone else's eyes. One person's heaven could be another's hell. Who are we to decide?"

He continued down the gallery and left through a set of high wooden doors. Buck and Betty followed, happy to leave the gaze of the painting.

When they reached the foyer they stopped a moment for Rathbone to speak a few kind words to a group of students gathered near the classrooms. They paid him great deference. The wide eyes and exaggerated nods. The nervous laughter. He came back to Buck and Betty and walked past them into the fading sunlight, waiting for them to follow.

The sun had dipped further in the horizon than Buck expected. It touched the top of the western treeline and threatened to vanish behind a wide stone building sitting just along the promenade. The shadows of everything grew long and thin.

Rathbone led them along a winding path that ran the length of the tower building, passing between a pair of English gardens and beneath a trellis draped in honeysuckle. He stopped a moment at the trellis and leaned over to smell the flowers. Betty pulled one from the vine and tore the bottom and licked the drop of nectar from the stamen. Rathbone watched her and smiled, then he pulled off one of his own. "Tastes like childhood, doesn't it?"

"Sweeter," Betty replied.

Rathbone nodded his head. "I would agree," he said. "Tell me, Miss Roy, how do you find our little campus?"

"It's beautiful."

"It didn't start that way. This hill was barren once, save for the cathedral and the tower we just visited. The land itself was all but spent. You could even call it abused. But over the many years of my life I have endeavored to make it beautiful. All the gardens and the trees. The little ponds. I have found that it is very possible to overcome rotten beginnings. It only takes time and a gentle patience."

Betty looked across the perfect gardens. She wanted to believe him.

"Strong foundations help," Rathbone continued, leading them

into the shadow of the great cathedral and stretching his arms to exaggerate the buildings scale. "And I could not have asked for a more potent one. A beacon you can see for miles."

"Well I've been looking at it for a long damn time," Buck said.

"Is that so?"

"You can see it from the parking lot of the Extra."

"How fortunate. Would it pain you to know that the building is something of a scam? A lie?"

"What do you mean?"

"Its age lends the illusion of a greater history. But its age is itself an illusion. There are, of course, no truly old buildings in America. How could there be? Those we have exist in mimickry. Their designs stolen from other, older places. This building is authentic only to itself. It's grand, to be sure. But it's only an echo of another age. An age that was itself an echo of something far older. One mimicking the next, on and on, until all we have are poor reflections. Copies of copies of copies. Beautiful perhaps, but quite empty. And always given to inevitable collapse."

Rathbone seemed quite pleased with himself. He stood again with his hands behind his back, rocking his weight on his heels. Behind him, Buck caught Betty's eye and made a yapping motion with his hand. Yap yap yap.

"Tolerated decay," Rathbone said sadly. "It's the best we can do."

They walked to the rear of the building where a garden of wildflowers blossomed in the lawn behind the cathedral. Petunias and geraniums overflowed the narrow lanes. The pale purple crocus with its golden anthers. Lily of the valley. Rathbone led them along a central path and took his time to regard the flowers as he walked.

"Nature, on the other hand, only perfects itself. It knows nothing of entropy. It builds its own cathedrals." He gestured to the flowers. "How could you improve upon any of these? What could we build that could ever compare?"

Buck was unimpressed. He checked his watch and made a long sigh. "You think we can speed this up?"

Rathbone smiled that familiar smile. Then he knelt down and began to dig at the heavy clay. When he stood back up he held a large, white worm cupped in his palm. It lay there like an exposed vein.

Betty stepped closer. As she watched, the thing in Rathbone's hand began to writhe and spin upon itself.

"Is that..."

"The specimen you wanted to see. Something small but wondrous, and to which we have no true equivalent. Perhaps a protozoa. A paramecium. It is a humble thing. Possessed of no purpose but its own vitality, but that alone is very, very special. Observe it long enough and you can see the manner in which it multiplies. I believe you would find it quite familiar. Dr Vivet became quite enamored with them, as you can imagine. They became his model organism. His white rat." He held it out further for Betty to see. "And upon this rock..."

It continued to coil and spin in Rathbone's hand, but its movements turned more violent and soon it spasmed and went still. Rathbone let the thing drop back to the earth and when it landed it barely had any substance. Less still a moment later, and as Betty watched, it dissolved to nothing at all.

"Stability will always be a problem," Rathbone said. "I've sown medium into the soil, which helps. But they were not made for this world."

"You made them?" Betty asked.

"No, my dear. I found them and brought them here."

"From where?"

Rathbone took the pocket square from his jacket and wiped the clay from his hands. "A dream," he said. "Where else would you find something so magnificent?"

He looked up to see how low the sun had fallen. Then he walked to a series of white enameled benches near the garden's edge. "Please sit," he said. "I could use a moment to rest."

Buck looked at the peaceful garden and the smiling face of Rathbone. "You want to rest?" he said. "There's a monster hunting us and you want to sit here and relax?"

Rathbone pointed far up toward the cathedral spire to the great stained glass window, visible there just above the highest eave. "I fully expect the doctor to arrive at sundown. And we'll be up there when he comes. Quite safe. I have something prepared."

"What, like a trap?"

"Something like that, yes. Believe me, Mr Vincent, I want it captured just as badly as you want to be rid of it. Perhaps even moreso."

"I doubt that."

"Well then lets say our desires are equal," Rathbone said. "Now please, sit."

He stood there with his hand outstretched, gesturing to the opposite bench. Buck and Betty looked at one another, then sat. Rathbone sat as well.

Buck thought he saw the iron bench sag beneath the old man's weight. "What the hell?" he muttered.

Rathbone didn't hear him. He just sat at the edge of the bench and folded his hands and watched over the garden. "Too much walking for this old man," he said. "Of course they've offered to get me some sort of electric wheelchair for my tours around the grounds, but I won't hear of it. Dignity is very important when you're my age. Lose a shred of it and you don't get it back."

"What did you mean about finding that worm in a dream?" Betty said.

"I meant exactly what I said. I found it in a dream."

Rathbone checked his watch again, then he looked up to Betty and smiled. "I've dreamt of the same place my entire life," he said. "It has formed the basis of my work, and the research of this University. A constant dream. A wilderness of life."

Betty listened with her arms folded. Buck watched the sun begin to vanish behind the trees.

"You don't believe me?"

Betty shook her head.

Rathbone laughed. "Nor should you," he said. "It is unbelievable. But it is quite true. Always the same dream." He looked over the garden again, as if he were remembering something vital. Then he turned to Betty. "It frightened me so terribly as a child," he said. "I would be afraid of sleep. Afraid of the night. You can imagine the toll that took. Nearly unbearable. My only relief came when I would draw the things I'd see. I would catalog them, like a young Grinnell, and they became creatures to be studied, not feared. I filled notebook after notebook, and when my mother found them beneath my bed she called them blasphemous. And I her little devil.

She tore them all to pieces and locked me in a closet for two full days with no water or food. I was seven years old."

"Jesus," Betty whispered.

"There is nothing on Earth worse than a cruel mother, Miss Roy. I'm sure you would agree."

Betty just looked at him. Her gaze seemed far away.

Rathbone smiled again. "She wanted to close the door that I had opened," he said. "And she nearly exhausted the pharmaco-poeia of the day in her pursuits. Heavy, heavy medication. Sedatives mostly. Laudanum, barbital, morphine... Treatments of every sort to quiet my unquiet mind. It was all too much to give a child, of course, but my mother was relentless. All the more so when her remedies proved effective. The haze I was kept in swallowed up the dreams. And most of my childhood as well. In my moments of lucidity I remember begging God for a better brain. How mine was clearly broken."

"That's awful," Betty said.

Buck rolled his eyes.

"It is awful. But great things can come from foulness. Think of these lovely flowers. The death they grow in. The decomposition. I credit those early years with my later obsessions in mapping the brain. Just where did those dreams come from? In which fold did they reside?"

Again, he turned to the flower garden. As though whatever memories he conjured needed a counterpoint. He seemed to find one in the purple verbena as it drifted in the wind.

"The drugs grew less effective as I aged," he said at last. "And I became quite addicted. Of course I did. What other outcome could there have been? My life seemed surrendered to the drugs and once I finally purged them from my life I began to have my dreams again. Little glimpses haunting me. And soon the dam burst and I was swallowed up. But there was no one to tear up the drawings this time, I made sure of that, and over the years I learned to endure the visions. I learned to love them, actually. To accept that place as a second home. What choice did I have? I traveled there every night, mapping it like an early explorer. I still do."

"And that thing came from your dream?"

"It did."

"How?"

"Patience and fortitude. And no small amount of money."

Rathbone looked up to the sky. The sun had now vanished fully beneath the treeline and the sky turned a deeper shade of blue. "Why don't I show you?" he said. "But please, no photographs."

He led them through the garden and across the perfectly manicured lawn behind the cathedral. A wide set of ironclad doors stood at the building's base. On the wall beside them was a white box with a small red light and Rathbone walked to it and touched a keycard from his pocket and waited for the light to turn green. When it did, he pushed the doors open and led them inside.

Buck expected to find more cold, stone hallways and high pitched ceilings. Maybe some gargoyles to boot. Instead, he was greeted by a glass-walled hallway with open laboratories branching off in every direction. He saw men and women in hazmat suits standing amidst spinning machinery and cooling clouds of nitrogen. Blue oxygen tubes lined the ceiling beside coils of electrical conduit. Airlocks separated all the doors.

"Whoa," Buck said.

"You were expecting Notre Dame?" Rathbone joked.

"Yeah I guess I was."

"I've left a few of the more sacred spaces alone, but most of these floors have been converted to the laboratories you see. Much of our research deals with the electromagnetic spectrum and frequency generation. Our primitive attempts at hearing what cannot be heard. Seeing what cannot be seen. A tiny window to my great paradise."

"You can see into your dreams?"

"In a matter of speaking. My dreams plotted our course, but the place we explore is quite real."

"And those things in the garden…"

"Tiny inhabitants. Nearly insignificant. But we extracted and cultivated them. Leading eventually to Dr Vivet's work in regeneration. Just a taste of the knowledge we have yet to uncover. A marker on the greater path of our curriculum."

"And what is that?"

"Transcendence. Though I would never say that to the board."

He smiled as he said this, as though it were a joke. Betty smiled along with him, but the more she considered his words the more troubled she grew. The laboratories they passed began to trouble her as well. One bathed in hard blue light held nothing but a great pillar ringed in small glass tubes, each holding something small, pale, and organic. Biohazard symbols covered the walls. Another housed two vast spheres of metal with a thick arc of purple electricity held between them. Betty recognized it immediately. She elbowed Buck.

"Looks like that thing that blew up the lab," he said under his breath.

Betty nodded. "Just bigger," she said.

They stood to watch. The arcing beam focussed into a soft beam of light just as a bell jar was being raised on a piston in the floor. Some animal thrashed within the bell jar, too fast for their eyes to understand.

"This way please," Rathbone said, his voice slightly raised.

They looked to the end of the hall where Rathbone stood at the doors of an elevator.

"This is some spooky shit," Buck whispered.

"You think we can get out?"

Buck stole a glance at the door they entered. A small red light glowed there on the reader. "Not without a card."

"Damn."

"Yeah."

They walked to the elevator and stepped in just as the door began to close.

"Time is not our ally tonight," Rathbone said as he pressed the button for the top floor. "I'm afraid the doctor will be quite punctual. Even if we are not."

XIV

THE NEW WIFE

THE TOP FLOOR of the cathedral looked nothing like the first. It was as if the elevator had taken them back in time. The doors opened and Rathbone led them into a vast room dominated by the great stained glass window they had seen from the garden. Shades of pink and red all spun together against a field of blue. Thick veins of lead. The pristine image of the rose was now distorted, almost abstract, and what little light remained in the day spilled through its petals and cast a red glow across the stone floor.

Rathbone led them to a high backed chair placed in the center of the room. A great tangle of thick black cables surrounded the chair and they carefully stepped between them as they approached. Betty stopped a moment and bent down to look at the small silver spheres at each cable's end.

"Stasis generators," Rathbone said. "Once activated they have the unusual property of slowing inertia. I've also installed a resonator below the floor which will be quite unpleasant for the doctor."

"Unpleasant?" Buck said.

"It is the inverse of the origin frequency. It will be anathema to him."

Buck looked suspicious.

"Kryptonite," Betty said. "It's like kryptonite."

"And what's with the chair?"

"That's where you'll be seated, Mr Vincent."

"Here?"

"Yes."

"In the center of the goddamn room? Like bait?"

"I'm afraid so, but you will be quite safe behind the stasis field. Now, if you please."

Rathbone made a little bow and gestured to the chair. Buck looked at it and sighed, then stepped over the cables and sat down. Rathbone patted the chair then walked a flight of stairs to a landing just at the base of the rose window. A large door sat in the wall near the window's base and Rathbone went to it and flipped the latch and pushed it open.

"I'd prefer the doctor not shatter my window when he arrives," Rathbone called down to them.

Betty walked back toward the elevator. There was a small desk and a rolling chair in an alcove near the bay doors and she started toward them when Buck called out her name. He made a smoking gesture with his fingers to his lips and she pulled the pack and lighter from her pocket and tossed them to him. Rathbone cast him a dirty look, but Buck just shrugged it off. He took a long drag then kept the cigarette at the corner of his mouth while he checked the revolver.

"So you drugged me last night."

Rathbone had descended the stairs and was checking the wire connections at a terminal beside the elevator bay. He spoke to Buck over his shoulder. "I saw no other way of keeping you safe," he said. "You were a little too drunk for reasonable conversation."

"So my hangover this morning wasn't from the booze. It was from whatever you gave me."

"I'd say it was likely a combination."

Buck considered this. He took another drag then asked Rathbone if he had anything to drink. Something to help pass the time. Maybe a Manhattan.

Rathbone turned from the terminal and smiled. He checked his watch again, then casually flipped a switch on the console.

The air immediately stank of ozone. A sound like thunder overhead as the small spheres emitted a simultaneous spark then fired a string of electricity that connected them to the matching configuration bolted along the floor. In a moment the electricity resolved itself to a dimly glowing field that surrounded Buck entirely. He could feel the hum of it in the air. It made his hair stand on end. His teeth ached.

"Christ!" he yelled. "You could have warned me."

Rathbone simply held a finger up to Buck, as though telling him to wait a moment, that he wouldn't take long. His smile was gone.

Betty walked to the other side of the energy field, facing Buck. The purple light rippled through the air and cast its glow across her skin. She could feel the pressure change in the air. Everything seemed to hum.

"Wild," she said.

Buck was looking over her shoulder, watching Rathbone as he approached. How the old man seemed to have straightened himself. How the steps seemed confident and fast. And that look on his face...

Betty saw the change come over Buck. She saw his eyes go wide. Saw his mouth open to scream. She turned in time to see Rathbone running toward her. He moved so fast she couldn't understand it. Like a young man, an athlete. She could hear Buck screaming and then Rathbone's face was right in front of her and then she was on the floor. It took less than a second. She looked up and saw how close she was to the elevator doors, but it didn't make any sense unless he had thrown her across the room. She had a moment to realize it was exactly what happened before he was on her again, only now he held her by the throat. She clawed at his fingers with both hands. She felt her body raise up and suddenly her feet weren't touching the floor and she couldn't understand that either. It all happened too fast. One hand around her neck and the other grabbing the elevator doors, prying them open. She could see the darkness of the open shaft. Good god. She pulled at his fingers, trying to pry them from her neck. Each was held like steel. She screamed out for Buck, again and again, and Rathbone squeezed her neck even tighter. She struck out toward his face, hitting something she couldn't see. It felt like his jaw. She hit him again, and again. With the third punch she felt something pop in her hand and the pain of it shot down her arm but she did not stop. Rathbone's glasses went flying. His grip did not loosen at all. If anything the violence and pain in her eyes seemed to excite him further. He held the elevator door open and smiled at her and then she saw darkness and nothing else.

Buck was screaming from behind the energy field. Every time he tried to breach it he felt the resistance of the electricity. He tried reaching out to one of the emitters on the floor, but found it impossible. He stood and watched Rathbone carry Betty halfway through the elevator doors and he screamed again and found the revolver tucked into his pants and pulled it out and sighted it. He shouted Rathbone's name, hoping for a clear shot, but the man didn't turn so Buck said to hell with it and pulled the trigger. The gun recoiled but he was ready for it. He sighted again and fired. Two shots in quick succession. Both aimed as far from Betty as he could manage. The sound was explosive. It careened off the stone walls and floors and for a moment the whole world went perfectly silent. Rathbone froze. He turned toward Buck and the smile was still on his face. Without looking he made a sweeping move with his arm and flung Betty down the open elevator shaft and then stood and smoothed out his suit.

Buck screamed and fired again and again and again.

Rathbone ran a hand through his stark white hair and looked around for his glasses. He found them lying a short distance away and reached down and picked them up and checked the lenses against the light. He put them on and walked toward Buck and it was only when Rathbone stood at the far edge of the perimeter that Buck saw all five bullets caught in the energy field, hanging motionless in the air.

"Those would have fallen right over my heart," Rathbone said. "You're quite the shot Mr Vincent."

"What did you do? You son of a bitch what did you do!"

Rathbone waved away the words. "Be calm," he said. "It's almost over."

Betty's camera lay on its side just beyond the elevator doors. Buck could not stop staring at it. He clenched the gun in his hands and he screamed out Rathbone's name, but the man ignored it as if Buck had said nothing at all. He simply walked a slow circle around the room. Hands held politely behind his back. Eyes never leaving the upper door.

Buck picked up the chair and raised it high above his head and brought it smashing back down to the floor. He felt something crack beneath the leather. He raised it again and brought it down again and Rathbone finally turned from the door to watch.

"Mr Vincent what on earth are you doing?"

Buck brought the chair down once more and finally the internal frame split and he pulled the leather off and took one of the legs and held it like a baseball bat. He squared up to the closest electrical node and swung the leg down high over his head, aiming for the cable. He swung with all his strength, but as soon as the chair leg breached the energy field it held there as if caught. Buck could see the momentum of it still moving downward, but it was slow as pitch. He let go.

Rathbone just shook his head. He stayed there with his hands folded behind his back for a long moment, then turned back to the door. Buck watched him with a dark anger he didn't think he had ever felt. He only wanted to scream. And when a scream did fill the room he thought at first it had come from his own throat.

Then he saw the figure limping through the upper door.

Dr Vivet, or what remained of Dr Vivet, stood there holding the edge of the frame. His weight seemed fully pressed against it, as if he had no strength to stand on his own. He was naked, nearly skeletal, with his stomach puckered in below the ribs. Deep bite marks covered his neck and most of the muscle in his shoulder had been chewed away. He let go of the door and fell forward into the

room, but his body did not hit the floor. It sagged low and stopped
as though held by something beyond the frame and in a moment
that thing stepped forward and Buck saw that they were attached
at the hip.

Rathbone took a step backward. Then another.

What flesh it had was drawn tight across a pointed frame of bone.
Like silk wrapping a bundle of sticks. There seemed little order to
the joints besides symmetry and from its shoulders sprouted one
pair of bristled limbs and from its hips sprouted another. Much of
the muscle seemed torn and exposed to the ligament, as though it
had grown too fast for its own anatomy. If this caused the creature
pain it showed no sign. It ducked below the doorframe and crawled
to the bottom edge of the rose window and perched there, dragging
Dr Vivet as it went. When it stopped, the doctor sagged downward
to expose the cavity blown out of the back of his skull. He held out
his bony arms and hugged himself to the creature. It watched him
with all of its white balled eyes and snapped its jaws at him like a
wolf. Then it turned to Buck and began to growl.

Of course he wet himself. He had fallen backward and just sat
on the floor. Too afraid to look and too afraid to look away.

Rathbone took another step back. "Doctor Vivet," he called.
"What a pleasure."

The sallow face of the doctor stared at Rathbone. He moved his
jaws up and down to speak but his mouth could form no words.

The creature only stared at Buck. It arched its back and gripped
the ledge and began to shift its weight like a cat about to pounce.
First to one side, then the other. It salivated as it did so. Its eyes
rolling in the sockets. It dug its bone claws into the ledge then leapt

screeching out into the void. Falling toward buck like something from a nightmare. Its wet lips pulled far back. All teeth and gums. And those eyes. The claws extending out from the fingers and they reached the energy field first and slid into it from the force behind them. The whole creature then plunged into the field and slowed down like falling into glue until it finally froze in midair. A single claw pierced the center where Buck sat on the ground.

Rathbone ran to the terminal and pressed a sequence of buttons and a deep, throbbing sound began to emanate throughout the room. As if a great turbine had just begun its first slow rotations beneath the floor. Buck could feel it in his chest. A few more adjustments and the noise sped up, but its pitch deepened further and further until finally there was no sound at all. Just a steady vibration throughout the room. The broken chair seemed to shift around the floor on its own. The lights began to flicker.

The creature held still in the air but as the vibrations grew Buck could see that it was affected by them far more than anything else in the room. It almost lost focus as he watched it. As if there were two of them overlaid a few inches apart and he was seeing a flicker between them. Doctor Vivet was unaffected and the last foot of skin and bone that held the two together began to tear and in a moment they were split apart entirely. A rippling sphere of blood grew between them in the air.

Rathbone walked from the terminal and crossed the room and stood at the edge of the energy field. He shook his head in wonder. "She's magnificent," he said. "Absolutely magnificent. And all from a tiny worm. Just imagine what something greater could produce. Just think of it. And there are far greater things in the dream. Gods.

You couldn't even imagine."

Buck was so disgusted by the thing facing him that he barely noticed the elevator door as it began to open. Rathbone didn't notice it at all. One inch, then another. Fingers, then a hand, and soon Betty had her entire shoulder wedged into the gap. She braced herself and pried the doors open just enough for the rest of her body and slid through and spilled out onto the floor.

Rathbone heard the noise she made. He turned and clicked his tongue. "My goodness," he said. "Aren't you a slippery little thing?"

Betty stood as he crossed the room. Her face was bloody and one arm was badly torn and hanging limp at her side. She took in the impossible scene before her and just shook her head.

"Betty!" Buck yelled. "Hot damn! Hot damn!" He actually jumped up and down.

She gave him a tired thumbs up, then spat blood on the ground. Rathbone walked a slow circle around the energy field. He seemed in no hurry at all.

"Exactly how would you like to die this time, Miss Roy? If the elevator shaft was unsuitable I could throw you from the edge of the building instead."

She took a step toward the terminal. "How about you go fuck yourself," she said. "How about that?"

"You tell him Betty!"

Rathbone stepped between them.

"I could feed you to the new Mrs Vivet if you would like. She would lick the meat right off your bones. Polish them clean. She comes from a place of hunger, you know. Hunger and pain."

Another step.

Buck's eyes went wide. He waved frantic at Betty and when she glanced at him he made a small nod with his head. He held up a finger.

"Or I could just choke you with my hands and watch your eyes go cold."

"You could stop talking for once," Betty said. "That would be nice."

She stopped a foot away from the terminal then looked at Buck from the corner of her eye. His finger was still in the air.

Rathbone took another step.

Then another.

His hands began to shake with excitement. "I'll show you the machine first," he said. "The one that links our worlds. I'll show you the things I've seen and you'll go so mad you'll eat your own tongue. That's what I'll do. That's just exactly what I'll do…"

Buck lowered his finger. He took one last look at the monster careening down on top of him and then he looked at Betty.

"Hey Rathbone," he said. "Hey. You hear me asshole? Don't you lay a goddamn finger on her. Don't even fucking think about it!"

Rathbone turned slowly to face Buck.

"Oh Mr Vincent, what do you have to threaten me with? You're absolutely nothing at all."

"Well I'm about to be a goddamn hero," Buck said, standing there in his wet pants. He looked at Betty, covered in blood and shaking her head at him. She was looking at Buck and then right behind him to the creature only inches away. He smiled at her and nodded. "Do it Betty."

Rathbone had just enough time to glance down at the five bullets pointing to his heart before Betty slammed her hand down on the button. The air hissed and popped and the energy field flickered out and the bullets flew into Rathbone's chest with an empty thud. Buck smiled and watched Rathbone fall. Then the creature collided with him. It had nowhere to go but forward, and Buck had nowhere to go at all.

He felt a strange pressure run the full length of his body. As if he had fallen into deep water. His chest compressed. He heard a sound like muffled screaming and his vision filled with a swirling mass of limbs and spines before resolving into darkness.

Darkness and silence.

A blooming light. Crest of the far horizon. Dead night sky bleeding into crimson. No stars at all. And below, a swirling ocean. Lidless eyes watching him. Jaws slowly working. Lips whose words he could not hear though the sound was beginning to form and the sky was shifting to a brighter red and all around the rising sounds of screams.

He gasped for air. He stood in the center of the cathedral room and Betty stared at him with her eyes huge and Rathbone lay motionless on the floor in front of him and the creature rolled over itself and collided with the far wall. The heavy thrumming noise still sounded from below and the creature still phased out of focus with the rhythm.

It turned and leered at him. Its lips pulled back to its eyes. It cried out into the room and Buck felt cold all over. He backed away. One step then another. And when his heel caught he thought it was on a cord but it was held in the bony hand of Dr Vivet. The dessicated man was just laying there bleeding and grinning at him like a skull. He moved his jaws toward Buck's leg and Buck tried to kick away from him but he lost his balance instead. He fell as the creature reared itself back from the other side of the room. It howled and leapt once more into the air.

Betty slammed her hand down on the button. The energy field cracked to life and caught the creature by two of its hind legs just as it reached out for Buck's neck. He pushed himself backward and kicked at Dr Vivet until he broke free. He stood and faced the creature as it struggled against the barrier like an animal in a trap.

"You ok?" Betty shouted.

Buck didn't know how to answer. The memory of that awful horizon was fresh in his mind. Clear as though it existed just beyond the cathedral wall. The sounds of it. Not to mention the things slathering and screaming at him on the floor.

"Peachy," he yelled back.

He limped over to Betty. Her camera sat on the stone floor just before the elevator and he picked it up and handed it to her.

"Can you use that with one hand?"

She smiled weakly. "I can try."

The creature screamed and screamed, but they ignored it.

"I thought you were dead."

Betty nodded to her bloody arm. "I caught the railing," she said. "Hurt like hell."

She held the camera to her eye and began taking photos. Buck smiled as the shutter clicked.

"It went right through you," Betty said. "Whatever that vibrating sound is seems to have done something to it."

"I still wouldn't get close."

Betty agreed. She walked around the creature and photographed it. At no time did it take its eyes from Buck.

"So now what the hell do we do with it?" he asked.

Betty shook her head. She saw the skeletal body of Dr Vivet and took a photo of him as well. Buck looked at the desk in the alcove near the elevator. On top of it was an old rotary phone.

"We could call the police," he said.

Betty looked up from her camera. "You know there's other reporters listening in on their scanners, right? You're gonna give up the exclusive."

Buck grinned to himself. "You've already got the exclusive."

"Give me another minute."

The creature scratched and clawed at the floor.

"Please, take your time."

When she ran through a few rolls of film she walked over to the desk and gave Buck a nod. He dialed the police while she sat on the edge of the table.

"Yes hello, I'd like to report a crime…"

The creature still stared at Buck though it seemed to have stopped its struggle. The energy field holding it made that gentle sizzle sound and the thrumming beneath the floor did not relent. Betty had nearly tuned it out.

"No, Brabane University. Yeah on top of the hill…"

That slow steady hum. How the creature seemed somehow dissolved by it. Less than real. She thought about how it passed through Buck and she shook her head and looked at the terminal.

"No, it wasn't a bear. Yes I'm sure. I know, but I'm sure…"

Lights flashed there on the console. Red then orange, red then orange. She wondered if they had been flashing the whole time. She didn't think so. She barely had time to wonder what it meant when she noticed the overhead lights beginning to dim.

"Buck…"

"Well its hard to describe. Just make sure you come with guns."

"Buck!"

He held the phone to his chest and turned. Betty nodded to the lights. "I think its losing power."

"Ah shit," Buck said. Then into the phone: "Send someone now!"

He slammed the handset on the receiver and watched the dimming lights. He heard the heavy thrumming begin to slow. The creature seemed to sharpen into focus as it did so.

"We're leaving," he said

"No shit."

He ran to Rathbone's body and reached into the mans pocket for the keycard. Rathbone laid there in a pool of blood, staring blindly at the ceiling.

Buck turned to go then stopped. He looked at Rathbone's face.

"Were his eyes open?"

Betty stood at the terminal, watching the flashing lights and trying to decipher the dials. "What?"

"Rathbone. Were his eyes open?"

"I don't know."

Buck looked at the body again. Was he grinning?

The thrumming sound slowed further and finally stopped. The creature shivered on the floor. It seemed invigorated. It cried out, but not in pain, and it turned its many eyes to Buck. It pulled against its trapped limbs, then began to gnaw at them.

Buck ran to the terminal and grabbed Betty by the wrist. She pulled her arm back and gave him a look and then grabbed one of the dials and turned it slightly. The hissing sound of the energy field grew louder. The air between the cathodes burned brighter and the creature bellowed into the room. It's skin started to blister.

"Call the elevator," Betty said.

Buck swiped the card and pressed the button and in a few moments the doors opened. Buck stood inside and held the door. Betty spun the dial as far as it would go and then ran to the elevator and hit the button and as the doors closed they watched the room fill with a pulsing violet light. They felt the heat of it. And as the elevator descended they heard a loud crack above them and the elevator cable snapped and the car fell the final story and crashed to the ground.

They lay there in the dust. One of the overhead fixtures had fallen from the frame and swung from the ceiling by a wire. They heard a heavy spooling sound on the elevator roof as the cables fell after them. Then silence.

"You alive Buck?"

"Yeah."

"Me too."

They heard a pleasant ding as the elevator doors opened. Then the screech of fire alarms. The laboratories had all gone dark. The hallway too. The only lights were emergency lights and they filled the place with shadows. Betty grabbed the railing and pulled herself to standing then reached down to help Buck. His leg was twisted beneath a fallen ceiling panel. It took both of them to pry it off.

"Your leg broken?" Betty said.

Buck groaned as he stood. "I don't think so."

"Good."

She grabbed his arm and tossed it over her shoulder and together they ran as fast as they could. It wasn't very fast. Some serpent shape moved behind the glass wall of a lab they passed. A chortling sound came in strange rhythm from another. Cracks forming in the glass.

They reached the door and Buck swiped the card he stole from Rathbone and they rushed out into the garden just as a heavy breaking sound, like stone hit with a hammer, came from the upper reaches of the cathedral. They jerked their heads upward just in time to watch the top of the building implode. The great rose window sucked into the room in an instant. The surrounding walls buckled right after. Stones grinding against themselves. The spired roof fell in a slow tumble, crumbling into the wreckage below.

They just sat in the grass and watched. The full moon gave them more than enough light to see the top half of the building collapse. Debris began to rain all around them. Shards of glass and bits of stone. In the distance they could see a crowd gathering in front of the building. Men and women in their colorful hazmat suits, holding their masks at their waists and watching.

"Good thing you got your photos," Buck said.

Betty straightened up. "Oh no," she said. "Oh shit. Shit shit shit."

"What?"

"The camera! Ah damn. I left it up there. And all the film. Ah goddamn it."

Buck felt the blood leave his face. "You're joking."

Betty watched him squirm.

"Yeah," she said. "I'm joking."

Buck fell backward on the grass. He thought about the awful thing Rathbone had dug up from the earth, but figured they were somewhere behind him. The night was cool and the sky clear and all the stars were out. He heard police sirens rising from the town below.

Betty was still looking up at the building when something caught her eye. Just a flicker of movement, up along the crumbled spire. She cocked her head and watched.

There, in the moonlight. Something crawling on the parapet. Shoulders heaving. Little pinpricks of light. It stopped and watched her.

She kicked Buck. He was pretending to snore. She kicked him again.

"It's still alive."

"What?"

She pointed up at the building, but Buck couldn't see anything and now she couldn't either.

"You're seeing things."

A deep howl sounded from the darkness of the rubble.

"Am I hearing things too?"

Buck pushed himself to his feet. He kept his eyes on the building. The sirens grew louder.

"Let's get to the road."

Betty nodded. Together they limped around the garden and past the corner of the building.

A heavy thud sounded in the garden behind them.

They turned and there was the creature though it was burned and charred and two of its hind limbs had been gnawed off into stumps. It howled again and its eyes bulged and its claws grew and it scuttled across the grass with slathering jaws.

They didn't spare it another look. They stumbled over each other and then ran like their bodies weren't as broken and bruised as they were. They felt the pound of it running behind them. Heard the snap of its jaws and its labored breath. They ran past the cathedral and across the sidewalk and into the road. Neither saw the car barrelling toward them. The polished chrome grill and the long pink hood and the fuzzy dice dangling from the rearview mirror.

Tires squealing on the road. A sickening crash.

They fell into the wet grass of the median. Chests pounding. They turned and looked at the road and the Cadillac there and the torn and twisted limbs of the creature crushed beneath its tires.

"Ho-ly shit!" a voice cried. "Ho-ly shit!"

Kip wrenched open his door and fell out onto the road, kicking himself away from the wreckage of the car and the twitching thing beneath it. The police scanner fell out of the car behind him, still chattering away.

XV

FRONT PAGE NEWS

BUCK ROLLED the Volvo into the parking lot of the Midnight Extra at a quarter to nine. He parked and sat a moment with his hands on the wheel. The edge of his reflection caught in the rearview mirror and he reached up and angled it so he could face himself. The black eye was fading. He ran a hand along his clean-shaven chin and thought he looked younger than he should have. Maybe it was the morning light. He took a second to admire his new gold watch, then he reached over and grabbed the fedora from the passenger seat and placed it on his head.

Betty was waiting for him in the hallway beside the newsroom. She stood looking at the gallery of old tabloid covers. One arm was in a sling and a bandage sat just above her left eye and Buck thought she looked like a soldier walking the halls of some battle-field hospital. She turned when she heard him approach.

"Nice hat," she said.

Buck did his best John Wayne nod. "How you feeling?"

"Not bad. They gave me some pills."

"That'll do it."

She gestured to the framed covers on the walls. "So which one's it going to be?"

Buck scanned the wall and sighed.

"I don't think it matters," he said. "Just pick one."

The cover in front of Betty showed a grainy black and white photo of two aliens holding hands with a young woman in a bikini top. The woman smiled suggestively and the aliens just watched expressionless from their rubber masks.

"I think this one can go."

"Alien Love Triangle? That's a classic."

"It's creepy."

Buck looked again. He really couldn't disagree. He held one side of the frame and Betty held the other and together they lifted it from the nail and sat it down and leaned it against the wall. Buck pried the staples out with his car key. Then he removed the foam backing and took out the old cover. He started to carefully roll it up then decided against it and just crumpled it into a ball.

Betty had the new cover all ready to go. Fresh off the press. She laid it into the empty frame and Buck put the foam backing in and pressed the staples into the old holes with his thumb. Betty helped lift it and together they sat the frame back on the nail.

Betty stepped back and cocked her head.

"It's a little crooked," she said.

Buck adjusted it as best he could, then stepped beside Betty and crossed his arms. "I wish that was the only thing wrong with it," he said.

"Hey it's your first cover in years, don't be too picky."

"I wouldn't really call this a cover."

"No?"

"No."

Buck shook his head. "Man I wish you hadn't taken that damn photo."

"I tried to hide it, you know. Janet insisted on seeing the contact sheets. I couldn't fend her off."

Buck sighed. "It's a good photo," he said. "Don't get me wrong."

"It's just not what you imagined."

"Not even a little."

Betty didn't disagree. She looked at the cover and shook her head. There lay the creature, stark in the camera flash, broken and bloody and crushed beneath the wheels of the pink Cadillac. Kip stood proudly above it with one leg propped on the twisted fender, curling his lip. Bold text covered the page:

ELVIS KILLS MUTANT WITH CADILLAC!

"The next one will be better," Betty said.

Buck smiled. "Next one?"

"Oh this is just the start. You know the mutant's body never made it to the medical examiner, right."

Buck just looked at her.

"I called this morning. I have a friend there."

"A source."

"What?"

"A source, not a friend. You're a journalist. You gotta start talking like one."

"Well my source tipped me off on a real scoop. How's that?"

"A little snarky, but better."

"Well she said that the mutant never made it to her office. No record of it at all. So that means the ambulance that recovered the body wasn't really an ambulance. So that's something huge right there. And Rathbone's body was never recovered. Neither was the doctor's."

"Oh boy."

The door at the end of the hallway opened and Kip burst through. "Man oh man," he said. "What a team! Like the damn Three Amigos!"

He looked at the framed cover on the wall and stood between Buck and Betty and wrapped his heavy arms across their shoulders.

"Or the Three Musketeers! What were their names? Huey and Louie and something? Ah hell it don't matter. What matters is that cover right there! Whoa boy. You two set 'em up and I knock 'em down. Real shame about Bessie, but she's in the shop. Company expense. That cover is solid gold and they know it. Worth the price of a fender."

He hugged them both close a moment then let them go and turned to Betty and lowered his voice. "And I'll tell you something Miss Roy, that is a damn fine photograph. You know what you're doing. A pro!"

He slapped Buck on the back. "And this ol' dog still has some hunt left in him! I tell you what." He reared back and made a howling noise and Buck and Betty couldn't help but smile.

"Even Janet had some great things to say about you two. Called me a lazy bum, but said you two were heros. An example for the rest of us scrubs."

"She what?"

"Well hell Buck, she'll tell you herself. Sent me out on a hunt for you two. Wants to talk."

He gave them another howl and then left through the opposite door.

Buck turned to Betty. "You ready for this?"

*   *   *

HER OFFICE was as rank as it had ever been. Maybe even worse. She held the glowing butt of one cigarette and used it to light the next. Buck almost expected her to light a third and keep it on standby. She offered him the pack and he said what the hell and took one and Betty did as well.

"We should get some champagne too," Buck said.

Janet just looked at him through the smoke. The latest issue was laid out on her desk. "And what would that be for, sweetie?"

He noticed the look on her face. The disappointment. That frozen frown.

"For the issue. Kip said…"

"Kip?" Janet said. "Well Kip can get all the champagne he wants. I'll buy him a case. If it wasn't for Kip there wouldn't have been any story at all."

Betty opened her mouth to speak and Janet saw her and held up the cigarette and glared at her, then she eased back into her seat.

"You've made up some whoppers in your day, Bucko, but this one might just top the pile. Mutants and doctors and foul experiments at a university. How could I run any of that? Do you know how much money the university brings to this town? And you want to smear them with lies?"

"They weren't lies," Betty managed.

"And you, missy. You think these boring photos of some monster model you scrapped together are going to cut it for this publication? Tabloid of the year, sweetie." She thumbed to the back wall. "Five years running. I swear if it wasn't for Kip saving the day I'd throw you both out on your butts."

Buck took a drag of his cigarette. He smiled. Janet saw it and had no reaction planned. She just sat there looking confused and suspicious.

"Betty needs a job," he said. "And you're gonna give her one."

"Excuse me?"

"You hired a part time intern, but what you got is a whip smart reporter and the best photographer on staff. She needs a job and a title and a real goddamn paycheck."

"You got some nerve Bucko."

"Matter of fact I think I need a raise too. It's been what, ten years? So yeah, I think I finally earned one. You do that and we'll keep doing this." He tapped on the cover. "We found a deep well here. Lots more meat on those bones. Enough for some more plaques on your wall. Maybe even a real one."

He took another drag of the cigarette then snubbed it out in the ashtray and stood. Betty did the same. He straightened out his coat and tipped his hat and turned and left. Janet called after them but they just kept walking.

*   *   *

BETTY HELD the storage door open while Buck got the Bigfoot costume from the trunk of his car. He came around the edge of the building with the furry suit balled in his arms. Crocodile Boy's head was balanced on top and Betty grabbed it before it fell.

Buck let the door close behind him then went to the coat rack to hang up the suit. Betty found Crocodile Boy's trunk still open on the floor. She placed the head gently inside then slid the trunk back under its shelf.

"You gonna put that watch in here too?" she asked.

Buck turned from the coat rack.

"I have no idea what you're talking about," he said.

Betty smiled and shook her head. "I can't believe you stole a dead man's watch."

"It's a Rolex," Buck said. "I can't believe you wouldn't."

"You're a creep."

"You're just jealous."

Betty gave him a look and went to the side door and held it open. Sunlight spilled into the room.

"You really need to clean this place out," Betty said.

Buck flipped off the lights and followed her. "Funny you should say that," he said as they walked toward the parking lot. "I've been thinking about that room a lot. You know, in light of everything that's happened. And I think there may be some mysteries in there after all. I mean, I've kept every object of any questionable origin I've ever come across. Things that people would swear had some curse or ghost or connection to the beyond. Most of them were more than happy to be rid of them. Others had a price and I usually paid it. Some I flat out stole. Point is, I got 'em so I could take a photo and print an article and head back to the bar. But now…"

"You might have a story right here and not even know it."

Buck nodded. "I might have a lot."

They went to the Volvo and sat together on the hood. The day was warm and lovely all around them. Blue sky and slow drifting clouds.

"You know one thing I can't shake?" Betty said. "Everything Rathbone said about his dreams and all that. Some other place. It was nonsense, right? He was messing around with genetics and whatever else and ended up making a monster… right?"

Buck thought about the red sky and the swirling ocean he had seen when the creature phased through him. The eyes and the teeth. He suddenly felt cold all over. His mouth went dry. He patted his jacket pocket without thinking, feeling for his flask.

"I don't know," he said at last. "I honestly don't know."

"Because if it's true…"

"Yeah."

"I mean, that changes things. That changes a whole lot. I can't even think about it."

Buck checked his pants pocket. He knew the flask wasn't there, but some tiny bit of hope in his brain thought it might just be. Betty saw him do it. She reached into her jacket pocket and pulled out a thin flask of her own. She held it up with two fingers and shook it.

"Hot damn," Buck said.

Betty unscrewed the lid and took a drink then handed it to Buck. "It's not champagne," she said.

"Good."

He took a drink and wiped his mouth then handed it back. He looked at the perfect June sky and felt the sun on his face.

Betty lit a cigarette and handed one to Buck. "I'm the one that got tossed down the elevator shaft, you know."

"And?"

"Well, if anyone should get the watch it's me."

Buck lit his cigarette and laughed. "You know it's broken, right?"

"Really?"

Buck nodded.

"It just points to midnight. No matter what I do. I set the time, wind it. Doesn't matter. It just finds its way back to midnight."

"So why the hell are you wearing it?"

"Because it's a gold watch."

"Well I get the next one."

"You think we're gonna find another gold watch?"

"Whatever it is. Next cool thing we find is mine. Deal?"

"Deal."

Betty took a drink from the flask and set it on the hood between them. Cars came and went from the lot.

In the distance, the remains of the cathedral poked out from a break in the treeline. Tiny shapes of workers walked along the crumbled spire. You could see them by the dots of their hard hats.

"Wonder what they're doing up there," Betty said.

"You're the one with the telescope lens."

"Telephoto," Betty said, sliding from the hood to grab her camera bag from the back seat.

"Hopefully they hit it with a wrecking ball," Buck said.

Betty lifted the camera to her eye and focussed the lens. In the far distance she could make out the workers as they made their way along the broken peak of the building. They surveyed the damage and kicked rubble over the sides and folded their arms and shook their heads. A foreman walked among them with another man at his side, tall and lean and darkly dressed. The foreman pointed to the space in the empty air where the spire had once stood and the tall man shook his head and pointed to a place far higher. The foreman scribbled notes on his clipboard and walked on.

The author would like to express his gratitude to Janet Lane and the hardworking staff of *The Midnight Extra*. This book would not have been possible without their support. He also wishes to thank Tim Thorne, Beth Newcome, Joe Tammariello, Katy Haas, Jeff Muster, Shane Hofeldt, Devin Montgomery, Ben Schuellein, Jane Grenier, Matt Bagwell, Alan Winslow, and Ryan VanDalinda for wading through the muck of early drafts and offering up their honest feedback. It means a lot.

MONSTER FANS!

Are You Ready for More

THRILLS
and
CHILLS?

BE SURE TO FOLLOW

THE
MIDNIGHT
EXTRA

ON

"Instagram"

Made in the USA
Monee, IL
26 March 2021